THE ARTIST SPOKE

Also by Ted Morrissey

WORKS OF FICTION
Mrs Saville
The Curvatures of Hurt
Crowsong for the Stricken
Weeping with an Ancient God
An Untimely Frost
Figures in Blue
Men of Winter

WORKS OF SCHOLARSHIP
A Concise Summary and Analysis
of The Mueller Report

Trauma Theory As a Method
for Understanding Literary Texts

The 'Beowulf' Poet and His Real Monsters

THE ARTIST SPOKE

TED MORRISSEY

A NOVEL

Twelve Winters Press

The Artist Spoke copyright © 2020 Ted Morrissey

This is a work of fiction. Names, characters, places, and incidents either are the product of the author's imagination or are used fictitiously. Any resemblance to actual persons, living or dead, events, or locales is entirely coincidental. All rights reserved. No part of this book may be used or reproduced in any manner whatsoever without written permission except in the case of brief quotations embodied in critical articles and reviews.

Published by Twelve Winters Press, a literary publisher.

P. O. Box 414 • Sherman, Illinois 62684-0414 • twelvewinters.com

The Artist Spoke was first published by Twelve Winters Press in 2020. It is also available in hardcover and digital editions.

Cover and interior page design by the author. Cover image is titled *Chicago 6b*.

Cover and interior art copyright © 2020 Ted Morrissey.

Author photo copyright © 2020 Ted Morrissey.

ISBN
978-1-7331949-3-8

Printed in the United States of America

ACKNOWLEDGMENTS

Excerpts from *The Artist Spoke* appeared in the following journals, in different form and (usually) under different titles: *Floyd County Moonshine* ("Meditations on the Word"), *Lakeview Journal* ("The Glance of Orpheus"), *Adelaide Magazine* ("The Glance of Orpheus II" and "Medieval Music from Midwestern Universities"), *Central American Literary Review* ("Madison"), and *Litbreak Magazine* ("The Artist Spoke"). I wrote this book in fits and starts, often losing my way, at one point abandoning it for nearly two years. The editors who saw something of value in the work and published pieces of it over time provided more encouragement than they can know. It is not an overstatement to say *The Artist Spoke* is their book too. All books are made of other books, but perhaps this one more than most. So much so that it's impossible to acknowledge all of its sources of inspiration, but I must name its fountainhead, Shelley Jackson's *Skin*.

for Melissa, always
and
for my mother, Jody Morrissey, 1930-2020
and especially
for all the readerless writers
who 'proceed from a reckless inner need'

THE ARTIST SPOKE

Well are you conscious, or haven't you knowledge, or haven't I said it, that every story has an ending and that's the he and the she of it. Look, look, the dark is coming.

— James Joyce

1

THE ISOLATION OF CONSPIRACY

Yes, it was a burden. That thought did cross my mind. There were other things in life. . . . But once the egg had come to me, it was impossible to imagine a life that didn't contain it.

— Shelley Jackson

Chicago 6

THE AUTHOR WAS DEAD—AND NOT IN A BARTHESIAN SENSE: actually, truly dead. At first he thought it was a hoax, maybe even one begun by the author herself. All manner of wild theories flashed through his head. He was on the train, speeding through winter-empty fields and tiny towns that appeared equally empty beyond the flashing crossing signals that blurred by his window. The train's wi-fi was spotty, probably due to the snow that was falling across the Midwest, a late storm that no one had predicted until a few days before, so he had difficulty trying to verify the tweet from @northerniowalit:

A small plane carrying @elizabethwinters_author has crashed – no survivors - #ElizWintersRevelation

When he saw the alert, he instinctively touched his left shoulder. He had the idea, but only for an instant, that the tattoo had vanished the moment Elizabeth Winters expired (if the tweet was true). It was the sort of thing that could happen in Elizabeth Winters's fiction. For the final hour of his ride he fruitlessly attempted to get additional information. Entering the city, the train crept through a series of tunnels and beneath overpasses of steel, rendering his devices all but useless, cutoff from the signals that seemed to fall from space.

When he arrived in the city the station was packed and had the frenetic energy of a mall at Christmastime. He'd brought only a backpack, which he slung over his shoulder, and he was able to maneuver through the crowded halls with relative ease. He thought he'd lost weight in recent weeks, and it was confirmed by the fact he had to hitch up his jeans every so often. There seemed to be an inordinate number of mothers with small children pulling their own colorful luggage, which would impede his progress until he could excuse himself around them. Another significant impediment: a group that must have been attending a medieval fair or something. They were gracelessly trying to maneuver through the crowded station while carrying blunted lances, pennants, decorated shields, and tall cone-shaped hennins with trailing veils. It was ridiculous, but he felt sympathy for them even in his irritation.

When he'd applied to be part of the author's latest literary project, he imagined Katie would apply too—and he envisioned their getting their words together and coming to Revelation together, forever having that common bond. But Katie was unimpressed by the author's project and had no interest in applying. She called it grandstanding, not writing, and said she was a publicity hound, not an artist. He liked to think that was the first sign of trouble for them, but while picking his way through the travelers and their wheeled luggage, trying to reach the escalator, he acknowledged there had been other suggestions, other hints. Signs or not, Katie had moved back to her apartment a month ago, and in the last week they'd only texted twice—the final exchange didn't include the customary endings lumu (love you, miss you) and lumu2.

A coffee shop on the upper street level nearly drew him inside with its fragrant appeal, maybe some aromatic African bean. He resisted, though, anxious to reach his hotel and hopefully find further news of Elizabeth Winters's accident. In his rushing he nearly ran into a woman—a mother—who had stopped to bun-

8

dle her daughters against the cold, two little redheaded girls, identical twins it would seem. All three looked at him like he'd intruded on a private moment, there in the very public space of the train station.

In the queue outside the station, waiting for a cab (with snow falling from the colorless patchwork of sky between the tall buildings), he heard a woman mention the author's death. He looked back along the line but couldn't identify the speaker, maybe the blonde in the white coat. He had a room at the Livingstone Hotel. It was still a few hours before Revelation at the university that was Elizabeth Winters's alma mater. There was little to do but wait. He felt the heaviness of his breakup with Katie grow heavier, like each falling flake of snow added a measurable weight to his blue mood—and if he stood still long enough he would be buried, a snowman of angst. A taxi for him pulled to the curb, and he got out of the storm as quickly as he could.

The woman at the Livingstone's front desk told him how fortunate he was because his room had a view of the lake, but when he pulled the cord, hand over hand, to raise the room's blinds (white snowlight flooding in), all he saw were buildings and the long, busy thoroughfare: vehicles, including many yellow taxis, moved in a continuous line through the slush. The snow obscured his view, yet not enough to hide an enormous lake, which must've been to his left. He moved a very neo-deco chair (work-zone-orange leather and blindingly bright chrome) so that he could get in the corner of the room, next to the picture window. If he put his face against the cold glass and strained to see as far to the left as humanly possible, he could view about an inch of marine-gray lake. So the front-desk woman wasn't lying. His guess was she'd never tried to view the lake from No. 824 herself; otherwise she wouldn't have reported his good fortune so cheerfully.

There was free wi-fi in the hotel lobby. He unpacked his tablet and went down to search the web for more details of Eliza-

9

beth Winters's alleged death. He was strangely unaffected by it, perhaps somewhat in shock, perhaps in literal disbelief.

The Livingstone's lobby was essentially a single large room, with the registration desk tucked into one corner, a coffee kiosk in another, then a bar and bistro taking up about half the area. There was a large fireplace (large fire currently roaring), a pair of red-baize billiard tables, and mismatched chairs, sofas, and ottomans, mostly in leather—it was the epitome of a cozy and eclectic setting. It effected the vibe from an earlier age of an inn for road-weary travelers. He purchased a glass of beer and sat in an overstuffed club chair. A window offered a view of the continuing winter storm.

The web now had numerous reports of the crash, a small private plane, in a remote spot in northern Iowa—even some major news outlets had picked up the story. But they were all reporting the same dearth of details. A few offered a makeshift obituary: avant-garde author, winner of the Calvino Prize for Experimental Fiction (actually, one of her most traditional pieces), originally from Evanston, Illinois, lived in Santa Rosa, California, with her long-time companion (a couple of sources described her as wife) Marian Tate, who also perished in the crash, it was presumed. Most of the stories included that Elizabeth Winters was traveling to reveal her latest work: a 753-word story known only as the project's title, Logos Alive.

He took a drink of beer and felt his shoulder through his shirt and sweater. He'd learned of Logos Alive from a student in his Tomorrow's Great Books seminar. They were reading Elizabeth Winters's *Orion*, her novel structured according to the principles of astral navigation which she had also published via mathematical language broadcast into outer space from the Hat Creek Observatory. Rumor had it that the Hat Creek edition had an epilogue which totally recast the mood of *Orion*, in retrospect—but the epilogue wasn't available in print on earth. The joke in seminar was that Elizabeth Winters would either spark an alien invasion or avert one—what other author could boast that sort of influence?

His seminar student had been checking out Elizabeth Winters's website before class and saw the CFF, the *call for flesh*. She was requesting 753 participants who would have a word (in some cases, a word plus punctuation) tattooed on their body (location, point size and font dictated by the author)—and also allow a subcutaneous chip to be implanted. As soon as class ended he went to his office and completed an application to participate. According to her website, Elizabeth Winters had written a short piece that 753 people would be part of, word by word. Only the bearers of the story would be given access to the narrative. He'd always felt a loss at not knowing the aliens' epilogue of *Orion*, and he didn't want to be left in the dark on Logos Alive. There was no explanation for the purpose of the subcutaneous chip.

He received a news alert on his phone that amended the earlier crash stories: Elizabeth Winters's companion, Marian Tate, was alive. She had flown ahead, to prepare for Revelation. Marian Tate's only comment, posted to the author's website, was that Revelation would proceed. He switched attention to his tablet but found nothing further.

He was keeping his phone close because he was hoping Katie would text to see if he arrived all right, or to say something about Elizabeth Winters's accident. But there was nothing. He wanted to text her, to pretend that he was just letting her know the news, in case she hadn't heard. He knew, however, how pathetic that would be.

I bet you're a Logos.

He turned in his chair, and the blond woman from the taxi queue, the one with the white coat, was standing there, the white coat draped over her arm.

Sorry, didn't mean to snoop, but Elizabeth's photo jumped out at me.

The news story he'd been skimming had a portrait of the author from the *Orion* jacket. Elizabeth Winters's red hair is swept from her face, and she's looking back at the camera, almost a smile on her red lips. It's okay—and, yeah, I'm a Logos. He patted his shoulder.

The woman touched her hip. She was wearing a gray wool skirt and a darker gray turtleneck sweater, black tights and boots. She was attractive behind a pair of glasses with blue frames. She was holding a drink (something amber, like whiskey and water). There was a ring on her left ring finger which may or may not have been a wedding ring.

The lobby had been filling up, and there were only a few open seats, including the chair adjacent to his. Would you like to . . . ? He gestured toward the chair.

She hesitated a second before folding her coat over the back of the chair and sitting. She placed her drink on the small side-table between their angled chairs, and offered her hand. I'm also Elizabeth but go by Beth.

Hi, Christopher . . . Chris. Her hand was cold but soft. So, you're staying here?

I had them take my luggage to my room. I hate to sound like an alcoholic but I really needed to have a drink and take a deep breath. I'm a little in shock. I can't believe she's gone. It doesn't seem real. I know that's a cliché, but it really doesn't.

I know. With her flair for publicity, I keep thinking it's a stunt, hoping—especially given the timing—but that'd be cruel of her.

It was noisy in the lobby and they had to lean toward each other to chat.

Beth sipped her drink. She glanced about the lobby. You think most of them are Logos?

Maybe. I suppose we'll find out in a few hours.

It is just a few hours away, isn't it? This isn't what I was expecting. This mood of mourning. It was supposed to be a celebration . . . of literature, of art . . . of life.

It may be yet. His voice held little conviction.

12

Thanks for offering me a sit. I'm going to my room—to freshen up, as they used to say in the movies. She stood with her drink and gathered her coat and purse. Maybe we can share a cab when it's time.

Great. He looked at his phone. So, we can meet in the lobby at . . . three?

Three then. They exchanged numbers, in case it'd be useful, then Beth headed toward the elevators. He appreciated the fact her coat was draped over her arm.

He began composing a text to Katie—he'd arrived on time in spite of the storm, had she heard about Elizabeth Winters?—but deleted it. The triteness of how Katie and he met was almost embarrassing. She was his teaching assistant but they were close in age. She was a bit older for a grad student, having taught junior high English for three years before quitting to work on her master's, and he had completed his doctorate and found a tenure-track position in the bare minimum of time. Katie finished her degree, with a specialization in rhetoric, and the university offered her a contractual job teaching first-year writing. They were suddenly colleagues, and they started seeing each other in the fall. They'd been all but living together for a while but Katie had kept her efficiency apartment near campus, mainly for appearance's sake, or so he used to think. Looking back, it was his suggesting (all right, maybe pressuring a bit) that she give up her place and move in with him in earnest that perhaps began the fissure. The argument over Logos Alive didn't so much broaden the fissure as shine a bright light that revealed its depth and breadth. One might say that he overreacted to Katie's rejection of Elizabeth Winters and her project, but he read it, even at the time, as a rejection of him, of *them*; so in that context his reaction was just about right.

He swallowed the last of the beer from his glass. He thought perhaps he should go to his room and rest before Revelation. Instead he ordered another glass, and pulled up one of his favorite Elizabeth Winters interviews: her *Rain Taxi* interview from a few years before. The waitress brought his beer, and he settled in with the author's wit and wisdom, and the thing he admired most: her artistic courage, her risk-taking. She said in the interview, I don't have much use for writers who play it safe. What's the point of telling a story that's been told a zillion times in the same way a zillion other storytellers have told it?

Around him there was the accoutrement of babbling voices, while billiard balls cracked together like unbreakable eggs colliding on the crimson baize—but he sank into the words of Elizabeth Winters, trickling across the quiet pond of his tablet.

When the old-fashioned letter had arrived from Elizabeth Winters and the Logos Alive project, he felt more anxiety, more excitement than he'd anticipated. Here was his *word*; here was *his* word. His word forever; his link to Elizabeth Winters and to Logos and all the other bearers of the story, the 752 others, from four continents, said the project's website. He had no other tattoos, would probably never have another—just this solitary word. A solitary word, to be inked into his skin, that would join him with so many others, all strangers, yet closer than family. Certainly closer now than Katie, who refused to join him in this act of commitment—to Elizabeth Winters, yes, to the project, yes; but to so much more: to a religion of literature, to undying faith in the well-chosen word: the word of mortals elevated to the divine by well-crafted order, by inspired, sweat-soaked design. He took a kitchen knife from the drawer and sliced open the envelope. He slid out the single sheet—good quality, cotton fiber, white—folded in thirds. He unfolded it.

pupils—

The word, a noun, and a mark of punctuation, an em dash. Pupils of the eye, or pupils of the classroom? Were they dilated or dedicated? Piercing or procrastinating? There was only one way

14

to know: wait for Revelation. The paper also instructed him of the location on his body, the point size range, the style of font, and the color: shoulder, 36-48, Times New Roman (or similar), black.

A week later, when the needle pierced his skin, there was pain, which he would forever associate with the pain of his disintegrating relationship with Katie. It was as if he'd been denying the pain, burying it; and the tattoo artist's needle lanced the place he'd been concealing it, allowing the pain to ooze from the wound. The next day, as the tattoo healed, an idea for a poem came to him. He hadn't written a poem in a long time, though it once was his main interest. He'd had several poems published in good journals and put together a book-length manuscript, titled "String Section," and went about looking for a publisher via contests and queries. During that time he was completing his doctorate and searching for a job. "String Section" garnered positive responses and even some praise but no offers of publication. Meanwhile, between dissertation writing and job hunting, he'd gotten out of the habit of writing poetry. His focus had become academic articles and conference papers, and notes for a scholarly book on the impact of late-twentieth-century technologies on literary style. The poem that came to him while his shoulder was still tender from the tattoo, eventually titled "Needling," was about release but not so much the release of pain over his breakup: more about his own release—from convention, from the purely academic track he'd found himself on, and from his belief that Katie was *the one.* He knew she wasn't, yet he missed her, or he missed someone in the role of Katie in his life—the role he desired her to play, not the interpretation that Katie had ultimately brought to the part. He thought of the poem's climactic lines:

> Steam poured forth from
> the geyser's eyes

but only the newly faithless
felt the warm spray as the
washing away of a caul.

"Needling" was a fairly long poem, eight stanzas, forty-eight lines. He sent it to a few journals, by itself, and it was picked up by *Chicago Review*. He'd been writing steadily since then, and had drafts of several poems he was preparing to send out. There was a sense of fulfillment to have something published, a sense of validation—but publication, even in a well-regarded journal, didn't mean that anyone read it beyond the editor and an assistant or two. It may have circulated just as successfully staying forever stored in the cloud, or a desk drawer.

He received an email—he couldn't help it: he wanted it to be from Katie—it wasn't. It was from the Logos project, Marian Tate specifically. The message was brief, written with the assumption that all the Logos participants had heard of the author's death; there was no mention of it, not directly. Marian Tate assured them that Revelation would take place, though not quite as planned. That was all. Well of course it wouldn't be as planned, with Elizabeth Winters not there, with her dead—but how far removed from the plan? A plan that had been impressively kept under lock and key, in an age when even the Pentagon's deepest secrets leached into tweets and leaked into wikis.

He looked up to see if the snowstorm had abated, but the view from the lobby window suggested that, if anything, it had intensified. He turned in his chair to look at the main entrance, and just then a couple was coming in from the cold. Their hats and coats were decorated with snow. They wore dark glasses and moved cautiously, snowblind, while the hotel-man struggled with their luggage that refused to roll because the wheels were clogged with slush.

Good. You're still here, Beth said as she took her previous spot in the chair. You saw the email? Her phone was still in hand.

16

Yes—nothing too . . . revelatory.

I wonder if we should go early. I bet Logos people are gathering already. Beth had her coat and purse.

You're probably right. Besides, who knows how long it may take, in this storm. Beth looked toward the front doors. The snowy couple was gone but their mess remained, melting on the floor. I have to go to my room for a minute, grab my coat and my badge. They'd been mailed plastic badges to present at the door for admission to Revelation.

I'll see about a cab. She was standing, preparing to put on her coat. She had a scarf and a knit hat, both red to accent the white coat.

O.k. He downed the rest of his beer. In the elevator he thought of inviting Beth to his room, of having sex with her, of the ring on her finger, of the betrayal, of the snow falling on the city, of the lake's cold gray water, of only being able to see an inch of the enormous lake. He thought of how often he fantasized about Katie before they started dating and he wondered if he would go back to fantasizing about her if they were in fact broken up. Would the fantasies be of the Katie he barely knew, of the teaching-assistant Katie, before they were a couple, or would they mainly be based on memories from when they were together? Memories edited and rewritten, rechoreographed and recalled again and again until they seemed to be true memories after all.

He returned to the lobby shortly. Beth was near the front doors. Just as he reached her the hotel employee poked his head inside, snow on his black hood, to inform them a taxi was there. Beth handed him a five-dollar bill as they passed through the doorway.

The cab was a red and white Prius, Downtown Driving Service, white letters on the red door, fire-engine red. The cabby was Indian or Pakistani perhaps. Beth and he began saying the college's address in unison; then they both stopped; then she completed the information. The cabby signaled and pulled into the crawling traffic.

He touched the credit-card reader on the back of the passenger seat. I got his. You tipped the guy at the hotel.

All right, but it's hardly an even trade. I'll keep a tab. She smiled—it was an attractive smile, warm, endearing, a smile that could broker treaties—before turning her attention to the window and the snow-covered city beyond. The sidewalks were not totally deserted but nearly so. From time to time one could see inside a diner or coffeeshop, and people were taking refuge there, bundled in coats and hats, and staring back at the winter storm only recently harassing them.

Sometimes he wondered if Katie was right, about Elizabeth Winters, that her cult literary fame was more effective imaging than writing talent. Katie made good points. Then he would recall his discovery of Elizabeth Winters—a story in an anthology, about a teenage boy struggling with his gender identity; it was titled "s/he." In the story, Tony (then Toni) is drowning in loneliness: it seems to be at the root of his confusion. The night Toni resolves to come out, to attend a house party in a neighboring town, she meets a young woman, Liz; and there is some chemistry between them, some attraction, but Toni knows the attraction is between *Tony* and Liz. Toni thought she had killed Tony, had driven a stake through his masculine heart, but apparently he lived on, calling out unhappily, bitterly.

Katie was still his teaching assistant when he read "s/he," and even though the plot of the story was remote in some ways (in other ways not remote at all), Elizabeth Winters's voice captivated him, at times plainspoken, at times lyrical—yet always harmonizing, always woofing and warping into a vibrant tapestry. The contributor's note mentioned *Orion*; he checked the time, just after six on a Friday. The indie bookstore was open until seven. It was a twenty-minute walk on a cool fall night, a night out of Bradbury.

There were only a few patrons in Finley's Books. It was a

18

long, narrow space, with mismatched chairs here and there, in an earlier day a drugstore. The patrons, a dozen or so in all, were reading—sitting sipping coffee or tea, reading, or standing deciding, reading. He decided Finley's was still a drugstore.

Contemporary fiction was toward the back in tall bookcases, two rows of them, standing solidly like sentinels, or like fortified barriers. He found *Orion*, the only copy, and turned around the end of a bookcase to return to the front of the store, ox-in-stall, and nearly tripped over a young woman seated on the floor, legs folded, reading.

Pardon me—. Katie?

My fault. I shouldn't be camped out here. She pointed to his book, her expression a question mark.

Elizabeth Winters. *Orion*. He nodded at the book in her lap.

Peter Cameron. *Coral Glynn*.

Katie wore a v-neck sweater, not revealing, not from a normal angle—but like this, the cleavage of her breasts arrested his gaze like a white spotlight. Her face and her breasts were the same plane. He forced his attention to the part in her hair but that was an odd posture too.

Ten minutes to close, forewarned the bookstore employee at the register.

Well, better make my purchase.

Me too, she said.

He thought he should offer her a hand up but in the instant he considered it she was already standing, fitting her purse over her shoulder. On the sidewalk, books in hands, sales receipts protruding like bookmarks, they said their goodbyes. The evening was young, they might have thought of something else to do—go for a coffee somewhere—both alone on a Friday night. It wouldn't be good for either of them, to be seen together, on a Friday night. That understanding hung about them in the air like a strong scent as they said their quick farewells.

They went opposite directions; after a few steps he risked a

19

glance over his shoulder at Katie's bluejeaned recession.

The street and sidewalk in front of the Dance Center were congested with taxis and Logos people, and two college workers in optic-yellow vests attempting to clear the slushy snow. It appeared at first a tableau of confusion, but when they exited the cab, they discovered that the Logos were being directed inside by a pair of young women holding the Center's doors, graduate students perhaps. It was more orderly than he'd assumed. Still, it took a few minutes of inching along with snow falling (now like fast, wet pellets) before Beth and he were inside. He'd noticed three or four news vans parked up the street. He wondered if the crews were there because of the literary event, or because of the author's death. He thought of Katie's argument, that Elizabeth Winters was a publicity hound, not an artist.

He and Beth were invited to hang their dripping coats on a rack down a side hall before going inside the auditorium, where their Logos tags directed them to specific seats, with the assistance of student ushers.

Inside the Center and auditorium was an odd mixture of jubilation and mourning, and a trace undercurrent of trepidation. He felt them all himself, but he didn't believe he was merely projecting them on the Logos crowd. It was the mourning that was the anticipated element, and as such it broke free here and there—in an emotional voice, a tear, or simply a look; or, for him, a leaden spasm in his gut. He recalled the night he read *Orion*, mesmerized by Elizabeth Winters's prose. He began reading the book around ten and finished it at two in the morning. He hadn't had a reading experience like that since high school, enthralled by a word-created world, enthralled, ensnared, enchanted. Both exhausted and elated, he slept in a space that was half his own and half that created by Elizabeth Winters and *Orion*. His dreams were wrapped up in the book. His chance encounter with Katie at the bookstore caused her, too, to inhabit that half real, half *Orion* world. He was thinking

20

of Katie when he woke, mid-morning sun angling between his bedroom curtains.

Inside the auditorium, Beth's and his seats were some distance apart. Before they separated Beth surprised him by reaching out and squeezing his hand. The unexpected gesture intensified his leaden feeling of loss. He hadn't cried for years, not since childhood, but on his way to his seat he felt tears beginning to well. He scratched his cheekbones as if they suddenly itched to staunch the estranged emotion.

His hair was wet from the snow and an icy drop fell to his cheek. It seemed there was a conspiracy in the universe, forces at work that desired him to shed a tear.

He took his seat, and in doing so he interrupted an intense conversation between the women who occupied the seats on either side of him. He apologized and tried to pick up the thread of their exchange. It seemed that one had heard a rumor about the Logos project: something was wrong—beyond the fact its author had died only hours before in a plane crash. The women—one thirtyish, the other maybe college age—were speculating what the problem may be, but it was only speculation. He turned his attention to the stage. The women attempted to continue talking but it was noisy in the auditorium, and without being able to lean toward each other it was too difficult.

The stage was a large black space, occupied only be a wooden, formal-looking podium which displayed the university's crest. He turned around in his seat to try to spot Beth, and it was easier than he'd expected. Several rows separated them, but she was looking directly at him when he suddenly spied her. Their eyes set upon one another. Beth smiled; he smiled, he hoped not awkwardly. Then he turned away, he hoped not awkwardly.

He looked again to the empty stage. He felt his shoulder where the tattoo was: pupils—. For these many months he'd wondered what sort of pupils. He'd read through Elizabeth Winters's books and stories searching for a clue and found not a single usage of the word. There were students and even a protégé; there were eyes and even an iris. But not one pupil.

When he first received his word he went to the OED. There was an older sense of pupil as orphan, a ward of the court. Or it could be the spot on an insect's wing. He wouldn't put it past Elizabeth Winters to use the word in one of these obscure ways, or in a way completely of her own invention. She was the sort of author who prompted new entries in lexicons. Urban Dictionary contained several of her usages.

He had the word tattooed on his shoulder but it had been imprinted on his conscious and unconscious minds even more profoundly. He was hyper-alert to it and it stood out in use all around him, in conversations, in advertisements, in print and on the web. Near the university a billboard began promoting a local optometrist who offered to school her patients' pupils for optimal eye health. In moments of quietude, while reading or commenting on student papers or simply walking, he would find himself reflecting on the word, as he saw it in the letter from Logos and as it appeared on his shoulder, in green-black ink, a serif font.

He found that not only had the word colonized his psyche, it had also begun to sprout a poem—and the poem was attempting to push through into the light of day. The poem emerged in bits and pieces over several weeks: a line or two in one sitting, a single word popping out unexpectedly during lunch, or he might awake to some punctuation scattered across his pillow. But the poem came—"Meditations on the Word"—and the process cured his obsession. He hadn't been fixated on the word since finishing the poem. He submitted it, along with four others, to a dozen journals, and the exorcism was complete.

On their first date he took Katie to the university's planetarium for a show that demonstrated astral navigation—how the ancient Egyptians, Greeks and Romans used it to travel the oceans and deserts, and how future space travelers will likely use astrocartography and gravitational topography to calculate their courses. The lights faded to black, their seats tilted backward, and the show began. In the bluish light of the projected nightsky Katie looked over and smiled at him. He'd wondered if the planetarium idea would be a bad one, especially for a first date, but the evening had been going well—a few laughs over drinks, then a nice dinner at the Greek place in town, Homer's, and a pleasant stroll to the planetarium.

They'd been colleagues less than two weeks when he gave into the crush he'd had on her for months, an attraction that was deemed inappropriate until she was offered the teaching position and graduated. Katie was traveling most of the summer, so he didn't have an opportunity to ask her out until she returned for the start of the fall semester. He spent the summer reading and writing; reading Elizabeth Winters and classics he had missed in spite of twenty years of voracious reading and a doctorate in English, the Russians especially, *Anna Karenina*, *Dead Souls*, *Notes from Underground*, *Fathers and Sons*; writing poetry, with a return to fixed forms, the sonnet, sestina, villanelle, and branching into Eastern forms, the pantoum, the haiku, the haibun. He took up gardening in pots on his apartment's balcony, tomatoes, peas, Brussels sprouts. He bought a secondhand telescope and gazed at constellations, Orion, Cassiopeia, Sagittarius, Ursa Major. And often he thought of Katie Sargent, traveling now but returning by summer's end to assume the role of colleague. He tried not to place too much emphasis on the fact, yet he couldn't help thinking of it, coming to him like a favorite song that is suddenly surprising you through the speakers in the grocery store, or thanks to someone's radio two cars over at the light: pleasant, unexpected and replete with special meaning. He missed the feeling of that summer—the summer of study, the summer of missing and wanting Katie. It had an almost monastic tinge in his memory: cleanliness, concentration, innocence, possibility. The feel of a beginning. He watched his

23

potted garden for signs of growth, the nubs of new shoots, the foreshadowing of flowers that foreshadowed fruit. Through his secondhand telescope he watched the cosmos with a near child-like sense of wonder. It was the summer of Comet Teffi, and he tracked the comet's progress, a massive frozen stone streaking through space ahead of its luminous stardust tail.

A woman walked onto the stage in the Dance Center. He recognized Marian Tate, Elizabeth Winters's longtime companion, the Alice B. Toklas to Elizabeth Winters's Gertrude Stein. She wore a black shawl over a purple dress. He suspected the shawl was a last-second accessory, a show of mourning likely borrowed from someone at the college. In addition to the emblem of bereavement, she had the shocked look of one who'd just lost the love of her life, suddenly, only hours before. She checked the podium's shelves for whatever she was going to need. She switched on the microphone and tapped it twice, then switched it off. She wasn't ready to begin, just preparing.

Around him the air was infused with chatter. He had the impression of turning the tuning knob on a radio as he shifted the filter of his listening focus. There was the bereavement channel, people expressing their tearful grief at the loss of the author. There was the academic channel, those debating the author's place in contemporary literature. There was the ecstatic channel, project participants who were coursing with adrenaline now that they were here and so close to learning the details of Logos. The narrative-speculation channel, guessing at the story the author would tell via the project. And the weather channel, people interested in the details of the snowstorm and how it would impact travel.

Amid all the frenetic conversations—all the energy and attention Elizabeth Winters had generated—he thought of Katie's pet criticism, that she was more grifter than gifted writer. But does a flare for publicity necessarily cancel genuine literary talent? In other times it was possible to be serious and popular (or at least notorious). Just last century there was Hemingway, Mailer, Kerouac, Capote . . . earlier Dickens, Wilder, Conan Doyle. He considered Hemingway's gigantic personality—the literal war stories, the African safaris, the Spanish bullfights, the boxing in Cuba, where he also fished for marlin. Norman Mailer's larger-than-life ego and his head-butting Gore Vidal due to a bad review and badgering him on *Dick Cavett*. There was Truman Capote, a regular on the *Carson Show* and holding court at Studio 54. Jack Kerouac reading from *On the Road* to Steve Allen's improvised jazz accompaniment on the piano, right there in every family's family room. Perhaps the patriarchy supported the idea that fame and talent were not mutually exclusive in men—but women, to be considered talented, must conform to some sort of Emily Dickinson-inspired model of artistic introversion. Or the Brontës, isolated on their windy and rain-soaked moors. They must be dignified, lady-like. He would have to hit Katie with that argument; it would put her on her heels for a moment—

Even as the idea sparked it was dowsed by the sullen recollection that Katie and he were through, and there would be no further debates—nor post-coital literary tête-à-tête. They used to enjoy discussing books and sharing gossip about their favorite authors in the halcyon time between sex and falling asleep. They seemed to agree on so much, other than Elizabeth Winters. It was like she was the other woman who came between them— but, no, really she was the well-aimed light which revealed the fissure in the foundation, the tiny crack in the keel, the nailhead in the tire tread, the faulty proof in the geometry problem. . . . His mind was aflame with metaphors.

Katie was critical of a lot of Elizabeth Winters's gimmicks, as she called them, but it was the author's reading in Sedona, Arizona, that she most frequently cited as evidence that Elizabeth Winters was more charlatan than serious author. The event was held at the Chapel of the Holy Cross, a Catholic place

25

of worship carved out of the region's distinctive reddish sandstone. Elizabeth Winters, wearing a pure white robe that made her resemble some kind of priestess, surrounded herself with New Age crystals and lighted candles. Instead of reading from her already published work, she appeared to do an improvised presentation, a narrative that seemed to draw from the real lives of people in the audience; about fifty people had come to the reading, according to reports. Elizabeth Winters was only a few minutes into her presentation when audience members began recognizing themselves in the story. As the author added more and more personal details, the level of discomfort in the chapel kept inching upward. Then, one by one, people began walking out of the reading, angry, hurt, insulted. Only about half of the audience stayed for the entire presentation. Had she discovered who was coming to the reading and researched their histories? Was it a kind of parlor trick based on careful observation as people filed into the chapel? Was there something more mystical at work? Or had Elizabeth Winters simply told tales that were common to humanity, like Joycean grand narratives, and audience members felt compelled to assign their own identities to the micro-stories? Elizabeth Winters, maybe relishing the air of mystery, never offered an explanation. Another mystery was how she convinced the local diocese to let her use the chapel in the first place.

He felt his phone's vibration alert in his pocket. Katie? It was Beth: Marian Tate doesn't appear too broken up.

He glanced behind and did something with his eyebrows to acknowledge her message; then texted, In shock? Grief can be a funny thing.

Texting about it made him feel grief's weight anew.

At that moment he was compelled to send another text: pupils--.

He'd broken protocol. Logos weren't supposed to share their word with anyone, with the exception of intimate partners of course, but certainly not other Logos. He didn't think Katie even knew his word. His getting the tattoo seemed to lock them on the rails to their estrangement. She expressed no curiosity about it. He never caught her sneaking a peek at his shoulder when he was dressing or undressing. Their lovemaking decreased in frequency (and even more quickly, intensity), and it was always in the dark, eventually a perfunctory part of the routine, like flossing one's teeth before bed.

When he looked back Beth's gaze was angled down, and his sense was that she was still contemplating his message, not wholly certain he'd just done what he did. He waited for her to look up. Perhaps it wasn't his own miniature revelation that mesmerized her. Perhaps she'd received a text from her husband, for example, something flirty and affectionate, offering her condolences and making sure she was all right—

Hello, Logos. Marian Tate had returned to the podium. She repeated herself to continue quieting the crowd, nearly eight hundred strong. If the death of Elizabeth Winters was some outrageous hoax, some elaborate prank to bring attention to her work, it certainly appeared that the author's wife was not let in on the conspiracy. She looked terrible. The black shawl she had pinned around her shoulders—to recast the otherwise festive outfit—accentuated her pallor. Even from the distance of the auditorium's fourteenth row, her eyes bespoke shock and grief. Her leaning on the podium may have been what kept her from collapsing altogether. Hello Logos, she repeated a third time, and the last of the crowd settled down to pin-drop silence. Thank you, thank you so much for being here and being a part of Elizabeth's project . . . for *being* the project.

One or two people applauded, then more, then it dwindled. He added to the tail end.

Many of you came great distances—Cameron Murphy from Toowoomba, Australia, I believe traveled the farthest—while others practically needed only step out their front door to be

27

here. But Logos represent four continents and forty-seven countries. Elizabeth was so pleased that there was a worldwide response to the call—

Marian Tate had to pause for a moment, overcome with emotion, but she quickly regained some composure.

Revelation was intended to be a celebration of literature but obviously circumstances have changed. Revelation will be both celebration and memorial.

Applause, uncertain, again.

As you are aware, Elizabeth has always explored the boundaries of communication, of narrative. Explored them and extended them. She extended them outward, to the heavens and beyond, with *Orion*. Her words, converted to the language of mathematics, are racing across the galaxy, bound for readers unknown, readers whom we cannot even conceive. Even Elizabeth, with all her brilliant imagination, couldn't conceive who the readers of *Orion* would someday be. In her Brandenburg poetry project Elizabeth stood at the old Gate and handed out lines of a poem written in Cold War-era invisible ink, along with instructions on how to reveal the words, and then tweet the line with hashtag BrandenburgPoemProject. Even though many of the lines never saw the light of Twitter, the poem that emerged was called by *Poets&Writers* one of the most beautiful and haunting pieces of poetry to be published in the century. Elizabeth knew, of course, there would be gaps in the text, but her genius relied on these gaps, these missing lines, to contribute to the meaning of the poem, to enrich the text in the absence of text.

He thought of Shakespeare's plays and their near total absence of stage directions, a vacuum that gave actors, directors, choreographers, costumers and set designers tremendous liberty to be creative in their interpretations and performances of the texts.

Marian Tate paused for a moment, then, As devotees of Eliz-

28

abeth you are familiar with these projects, and you may have known of Elizabeth's love affair with medieval literature. I'll wager you didn't know that she translated and published several pieces of Anglo-Saxon literature, parts of *Beowulf*, *The Wanderer*, *The Seafarer*, several enigmas . . . but always anonymously, sometimes to the editors' consternation, out of respect to the original anonymous Old English poets. These publications are listed in none of Elizabeth's bibliographies, by design.

His phone was in his hand so he felt the text alert. It was from Beth, just one word: radiant. For a second he thought she was commenting on Marian Tate, though radiant hardly worked; then he realized she'd revealed her Logos too. He glanced behind and she nodded. He wondered if some teacher's pupils were radiant in their brilliance, or if they were astronomy students learning how to calculate a radiant, or if radiant light caused someone's pupils to constrict. Probably their words were miles apart in Elizabeth Winters's text, but anything was possible.

. . . Revelation for many reasons. Now however not all can be revealed. For one, Elizabeth was so looking forward to you, the soul of Logos, finally being revealed to her, after the many months of taking applicants and screening them. I assure you Elizabeth read every word of the applicants' statements. As you know, there were well over a thousand applications, and from that group you seven-hundred, fifty-three were selected for Logos Alive. Let that sink in.

After a moment or two of silence someone began applauding, then a few others, until eventually all Logos were bringing their hands together, some whistling and shouting too. Martian Tate stepped from behind the podium and joined in the applause. He'd been registering the scent of wet wool for a while, someone's damp hat or scarf, and he knew that whenever he recalled this moment—this outpouring of love for Elizabeth Winters and her work—he would also recall the wet-wool scent.

She returned to the microphone as the Logos settled. She was quiet for a time, gathering her thoughts, or taking control of her emotions. Elizabeth, who always dreamed on the grandest scale, conceived of a way to tell this story, this novel, of which you are all an integral part, a way that would unfold across decades, across generations, more than a century in fact. I . . . I'm sorry, my apologies . . . I'm rambling. I was only to introduce Elizabeth and she was to reveal her masterplan. Allow me to try to explain in the simplest way—not for your benefit but for mine.

Marian Tate drank from a glass of water that had been on a shelf inside the podium, then began again.

You each bear a word, or possibly a word and a mark of punctuation. You seven-hundred, fifty-three Logos comprise the prologue of *The Isolation of Conspiracy* by Elizabeth Winters. But you are to be more than that, much more. You will have a chip implanted beneath your skin—excuse the comparison, but very much like the chips many of you have implanted in your beloved dogs and cats. However, these chips carry sections of the novel, approximately one-hundred words each. The chips are not to be read and the narrative assembled for more than a century, about one-hundred and ten to one-hundred, fifteen years. You would be privileged to read the prologue, but the text of the novel will not appear until after your demise, after mine—and long, long after Elizabeth's.

There was some quiet chatter among the Logos. He was trying to grasp what Marian Tate had just said. Questions were beginning to surface in the auditorium. . . .

She continued, The chips have been created by a company in Silicon Valley, and the data is encrypted so that it cannot be decoded prematurely. In one-hundred years the polymer that is key to blocking the reading will break down, releasing a unique isotropic signature which literary anthropologists will be able to locate so that Elizabeth's novel can be assembled and read. The end-of-life arrangements you make for retrieval of the chip are completely your decision. Elizabeth had total confidence in

30

your fidelity to the project. You must give it some thought. One can see that cremation, for instance, with the chip still implanted, would be problematic.

She paused a moment to allow the Logos to process Elizabeth Winters's grand design. Logos will carry a piece of *The Isolation of Conspiracy* to their final resting places, and in a century or so scientists will recover the chips, one by one, and the novel will be published—whatever published will mean in the twenty-second century. Marian Tate used the term isotropic signature, which sounded like a fancy phrase for radiation.

You may wonder, she said, Why not put the manuscript in some sort of literary trust, lock it away in a vault for a hundred years, with the instructions to publish it then? Elizabeth wanted you to be part of the story. She believes—believed . . . I'm sorry I keep forgetting she's gone. Elizabeth would shudder at my using that cliché.

A moment of lightness, some laughter.

She believed that by your bearing the story within you that you will transform it. Not literally, not that your DNA will rewrite the words—this isn't science fiction—rather, your stories, the stories of your lives will join with *Isolation*, and the book that will result from that joining will be far richer, far more complex. How this richness, this complexity will manifest, Elizabeth couldn't say, but she believed it. And she also believed that bearing the story will transform you—will enrich you, and, yes, complicate you. . . .

Logos Alive had already complicated him, revealing the fissure in his and Katie's relationship, amplifying their contrasting views of the world, of art. He imagined being the bearer of this unknowable story, of living year upon year with the knowledge that it was beneath his skin, connecting him with hundreds of others around the world—but also separating him from the rest of humanity. It was a reoccurring motif in Elizabeth Winters's work, especially *Orion*, and now the title of her final novel: the

31

isolating nature of a conspiracy.

There was something passing among the Logos in the auditorium, some reaction. He'd missed something.

. . . a vague understanding, Marian Tate was saying, but only Elizabeth knew the actual verbatim story. She had memorized it, word for word, and she was careful to delete all files—the Silicon Valley firm did that as well.

So not even the prologue can be reconstructed? He looked back at Beth in hopes that her expression would confirm what he thought Marian Tate was saying, but Beth was focused elsewhere.

My sincere wish is that this fact will not deter you from following through with your commitment to *The Isolation of Conspiracy* and to Elizabeth.

Here and there Logos were talking in low tones, but he didn't make out what anyone was saying.

Marian Tate took control of the room again. We want to follow through on Elizabeth's design as far as we are able. We will photograph your tattoo, then a medical professional will implant the chip, in your hip or forearm, I believe. We will send you the seven-hundred, fifty-three word-tattoos but unfortunately they will be jumbled. No doubt there will be many who will attempt to organize the prologue into the sequence Elizabeth intended. Who knows. It may become something of a competition.

He found he wasn't concerned about the long-term issue: the breakdown of the chip and its release of isotropic signals, which sounded like a euphemism for radiation, and the retrieval of the chip, its exhumation. Rather, he felt the return of his disappointment at not knowing the end of *Orion*, and now of being in the dark about all of *Isolation*. He would be the bearer, beyond his own death, of a story he had no way of knowing, a text more impenetrable to him than a fragment of some ancient artifact bearing a lost language.

Logos began questioning Marian Tate, not hostilely, not ag-

32

gressively, but intense in their need to know. They asked regarding the things he wondered about too, and she answered them but without any information she hadn't already shared. She appeared dazed and in shock, and to be doing the best she could to carry through with a plan she only partly understood herself. Around him Logos texted and tweeted and no doubt used myriad social media to send surreptitiously taken photos. They had agreed not to share their words with the world at large, but with Elizabeth Winters's death and the impaired project, people must've felt the rules had changed—or they simply couldn't resist sharing their small piece of the story—not the story Elizabeth Winters wrote but the story she had become.

He felt his text alert and started to open the message assuming it was from Beth, but the auditorium went silent for a moment when he saw that it was Katie who'd texted: You ok? He considered all sorts of responses including none at all. He thought he should wait a few hours at least. He looked up from his screen as if he was going to ignore it for now, but a half minute later he thumb-typed: A little stunned. Thanks for checking. And hit send.

He looked back at Beth, the backward glance of the guilty.

11

AMERICANA

Whatever work the contemporary American writer does must proceed from a reckless inner need. . . . Serious writing must nowadays be written for the sake of the art.

— William H. Gass

Chicago 9

THEY SHARED A CAB BACK TO THE LIVINGSTONE; BOTH WERE quiet. The snow had slowed but colder air was descending on the city with nightfall. The cabby was surprisingly cautious, respecting the treachery of the streets. For months he'd expected Revelation to be energizing and exhilarating. Now however he felt exhausted and not just physically: emotionally and spiritually too. It had taken another three hours for Revelation to conclude—photographing the words, one tattoo at a time, and implanting the chip. There were a few defectors among the Logos, people who declined being chipped, a combination of grief-strickenness and disappointment that so very little was revealed at Revelation, and perhaps simple fear at the idea of carrying a microchip in their body designed to become radioactive. For every defector there were dozens of Logos who offered to carry multiple chips—anything to bring Elizabeth Winters's grand plan, fractured though it be, to fruition.

The chip had been inserted at his hip. He sensed the insertion point. It didn't precisely sting but there was a heightened sensitivity, and a feeling of added weight—though that should be impossible. The chip itself weighed a breath of air more than nothing. It was as if he could feel the weight of Elizabeth Winters's words, as if their meaning—unknown to him—carried a physical impact in the world, like the weight of money in one's pocket: there was the coinage itself plus the weight of what the currency could buy. But also, too, it was like the weight of a secret on one's heart: the secret of love and longing for someone from whom that secret must forever be kept.

He glanced at Beth, whose alabaster face was queerly lit by the passing citylights, the reflected and refracted snowlight, and the cab's dashboard. She seemed almost a Warhol image, unmoving but always changing, not vivid hues, however, every color subdued and washed out, their energy ebbed nearing the end of a long day.

Are you hungry? Beth was looking at him looking at her.

Now that you mention it.

There's the Italian place next to the hotel, Sicilian more specifically.

Sounds fine.

They had the cabby drop them in front of the restaurant. One sensed that Isola di Sicily would normally be packed, reservations only, but the storm had kept people away, and the restaurant was only half filled. The hostess seated them in a candlelit corner. Beth held the hostess for a moment while she glanced at the wine list, and ordered a bottle of the house merlot. Is that all right? she asked him as the hostess departed. It's been one of those days and sometimes in these places it's a half hour before they get around to taking your order. Thirty minutes of pomp and circumstance.

They sat for a moment, perusing their menus, adjusting to the low lighting.

I feel funny, Beth said touching her forearm where they'd implanted the chip.

Funny how?

I don't know . . . strange. Like I can feel the words beneath my skin, moving or buzzing, like ants in a colony. I know ants don't buzz, but . . . not just under my skin though. My head feels funny, a little dizzy or something, like my thoughts are scattered.

38

We've had a lot to process in the last eight hours or so.

Do you feel strange too?

I know what you mean. I can sense the words also, or the weight of their meaning or something. It's hard to describe, an admission I'm reluctant to make.

He thought then, again—for he had been thinking of it almost constantly since receiving it—of Katie's message and what it may mean, in terms of their relationship. He believed they were through and was beginning to accept the idea, beginning to climb out of the funk he'd fallen into. He rationalized that he was better off without her. They didn't embrace the same foundational beliefs, and to be truly happy, in the long term, he needed to find someone with whom he connected at the deepest level of his being. It wasn't just the disagreement over Elizabeth Winters. He'd begun to accept that there were other issues too. Most profoundly perhaps, Katie expressed an agnostic position toward an all-powerful deity, a Christian deity, who created and ruled existence, and who provided for some sort of being beyond life; and Katie seemed to be leaning toward a more traditional way of thinking. He wouldn't be surprised if Katie returned to the church eventually, some denomination and manifestation of it. He, on the other hand, had dealt with his agnosticism in his late teens and early twenties before plunging headlong into atheism, with no thin residue of faith that he could ever return to, no god-based belief system.

The nearest he came was worshiping Elizabeth Winters and her writing.

But now, with that simple two-word question, materializing from the heavens—You ok?—he began to wonder if he-and-Katie was possible after all. Did she think so? Or at least wonder? Or was her text message pure human kindness? A message sent to a friend, likely a grieving friend. Nothing more.

Their waiter brought the house merlot and a basket of bread. While he opened the wine and poured it into their glasses, he

39

recited the special selections not on the menu. He went away to give them time to decide.

Beth set aside her menu. Are you planning on attending the memorial tomorrow?

I think so. I'll have to take a later train. I'll check to make sure that's possible. I teach on Mondays but luckily not until eleven. What about you?

I think so too. I wasn't planning on heading back until later anyway. I thought about hitting a bookstore or two while in the big city. I trust the snow will stop sometime.

Whom do you like to read besides Elizabeth Winters?

Beth smiled. I don't know many people who use whom in conversation—not many more who use it at all.

A habit I suppose from talking to my students. Teach by example.

I like it. It's like being in a Henry James story. To answer your question, I read all sorts of authors; in fact I'm all over the board, from Austen to Barth to Chandler. I like contemporary poetry too, especially haiku.

Interesting. What . . . *whom* are you reading at the moment?

A contemporary novelist, Peter Cameron, *Andorra.*

Do you write? I'm sorry. It feels like I'm interviewing you, or interrogating you.

It's o.k. . . . .

The waiter interrupted to take their order. Beth selected busiate with pesto Genovese; he ordered one of the specials, grilled sea bass tossed with pasta. They would both begin with the orange salad with fennel.

Yes, I write a little, she continued. I've been trying my hand at essay or memoir or something. I'm not quite sure what it is. She paused, sipped some merlot. I also write poetry, mainly haiku. In fact. . . . Beth took her purse from the back of her chair and pulled from its seemingly jumbled contents a small paperback book. She handed it across the table.

40

He read the cover by candlelight, *Frogpond*—a journal of haiku.

Heard of it?

I think I have, but I haven't read a copy. I tend to be a longer-form guy.

Turn to page twenty-two.

He did, and scanned the haiku. There was one by Elizabeth Winterberry, from Madison, Wisconsin. Elizabeth Winterberry.

Freaky isn't it. It's like being named Ernest Hemingwayfare or Oscar Wilder or something.

He read the haiku to himself: Barnwood drinks in the pain(t)—white—enflaming the maple forest. Nice. He handed her back *Frogpond*.

What about you? Do you write?

I have been. Poetry. I used to take it, and myself, pretty seriously. Then I stopped, but I've been back at it for a while. He took out his phone and navigated his way to *3Elements Review*, issue 9, and his poem "Parking Lot, 2 a.m." This one is pretty recent, came out a month ago. He handed Beth his phone.

She read aloud, "Parking Lot, 2 a.m." by Christopher Krafft. Nice double alliteration.

It's easy to remember, when someone hears it, but spelling it is a whole other story. The *k* in Krafft makes people want to spell Chris with a *K*—and no one gets the double-*f* right on the first try.

Well, I will, now. She read his poem. I like it. Especially the image of the yellow lines being chevrons pointing us one way then back the opposite. Don't I know that feeling. She drank from her merlot glass. Do you have a collection?

He thought a moment (and fully realized there was a string quartet playing music ambiently over a sound system). Yes and no. I have or maybe had a collection. I tried for a while to get it published, unsuccessfully; then I got sidetracked into academic writing. Recently I began writing poetry again. So, yes, that

41

manuscript still exists but I'm not sure if I want to send it out again or just concentrate on new work.

You should do both. Dust off that manuscript and send it back out into the world, and keep writing new poems. Absolutely that's what you should do.

Maybe. Sometimes I wonder what the point is—not the writing but the publishing. I mean, there are thousands of literary journals, print and online, publishing, what?, a million new stories and poems and essays a year, and indie presses churning out book after book—and who reads any of it? I don't know that a single person has read anything I've written, other than the editor who published it—and sometimes I'm not even sure about that.

I know what you mean. I get it.

It's like we're living in a new Dark Age, but not because of a lack of reading material or a lack of literacy, but a lack of interest in reading.

Beth said, But how many readers must a piece of writing have to make publishing it worthwhile? I'm a librarian, a keeper of books almost no one reads. Some items haven't been checked out or consulted in decades. Yet I believe they have value, that they should be kept, so that one day, maybe just a single person can find value in reading it, so that it can add meaning to their life. The worth of a piece of writing can't be determined by its number of readers. Surely not.

That's a good way of looking at it. We tend to apply an old, out-of-date measuringstick to reckon the quality of writing. In another time, if you wrote well, you were published and you were read. Literary agents would find you based on the quality of your work. Take you on, sell your work to a publisher, who would make your writing available to a wider readership. But that all changed in the last century. The number of large, money-making publishers dwindled to a handful, and all they were interested in was making money—and only mediocre

42

writers, or writers of mediocrity, could make a profit.

Right, I think only about two dozen authors account for more than eighty percent of book sales in the U.S. Something like that. It's nuts.

So nowadays having an agent and publishing with a large press are marks of mediocrity or perhaps chameleon-like conformity.

Perhaps it will change. Maybe this new Dark Age will yield eventually to a new Renaissance in reading.

Maybe that's what Elizabeth Winters is . . . was banking on. That her new book will come out in an age when people might actually read it and appreciate it.

We can hope, said Beth.

Maybe she broadcast *Orion* into space not in search of intelligent life, but more specifically in search of intelligent readers.

The waiter brought their orange salads.

After a minute or two Beth said, This is quite good, a little sweet but not overly so. The fennel keeps the sweetness in check I think.

He nodded in agreement.

I didn't realize how hungry I was.

He nodded again. Language-making seemed impeded. He had the sense that the food was nourishing Elizabeth Winters's words planted inside of him, like seedlings, precisely like seedlings, and their need for nourishment consumed all of his word-making energy. Their hunger raged like a parasite's. The locus of his hunger was not his hip, however; rather Elizabeth Winters's words seemed to weave a fine web which had enmeshed his soul like new skin.

He finished his salad, using the tines of his fork to capture the last few sunflower seeds. The energy for language-making returned to him. So tell me about this essay or memoir thing you've been writing.

Beth was still working on her salad. She washed down a bite

43

with a swallow of merlot. I think I'm struggling with it, with finding its form, because the subject is very personal—or it could be. When I try to distance myself from the subject, it becomes more of an essay. But invariably I slip back into a more private aspect, and the thing becomes more autobiographical.

It sounds like the thing wants to be more autobiography, more memoir—if it keeps tugging you in that direction.

I think you're right. I know you're right. But I'm afraid of that kind of exposure, of self-exposure, that kind of vulnerability. I'm afraid on several levels. At least, I guess, I'm not afraid to admit I'm afraid. That's something.

I must say, you've piqued my curiosity—but I don't want you to share anything that makes you uncomfortable.

I appreciate that. She moved her empty bowl aside and picked up a piece of bread to begin buttering it. It's weird but I feel this compulsion to tell all. Like Elizabeth Winters's words are taking up so much space inside of me they're forcing my own words to the surface. I can barely contain them—it's like having a full bladder or something. She smiled, a little embarrassed at her indelicate simile. Or maybe it's just the wine that wants me to talk. Maybe the grapes have fermented beyond mere alcohol into sodium pentothal.

Sometimes we just need to share. You know, catharsis. He drank some wine, whose arid qualities complemented the sweetness of the oranges in the salad. Perhaps that's what I like about poetry. Its elliptical nature means you don't have to confront issues head-on. Maybe I'm a little afraid of self-exposure too.

Beth seemed to consider what she felt compelled to say. Candlelight played on her face and the lenses of her glasses, coruscating to and fro as if animation of her vacillating deliberations.

The waiter brought their meals.

Saved by the busiate, she said.

At a nearby table a mother was seated with her two young

44

daughters, it appeared, and her children couldn't find anything on the menu to their liking. He recalled his own pickiness as a child, so he felt sympathy for both the exhausted mother and for her fussy daughters.

As they ate there was no further discussion of Beth's confessional urges. Instead the conversation turned to Elizabeth Winters and her work, how they each discovered her, and they recited or described their favorite passages. They both loved the Orphic fountain scene in *Orion*, a scene that manages to be both foreshadowing and redherring. They spoke of other writers and poets they admired. Beth had focused her senior thesis as an undergrad on the poetry of Harrison Gale.

No way. I devoted most of a chapter of my dissertation to A. E. Wilson. Gale and Wilson were—

Brother and sister. I love Wilson too. I was going to include a couple of her poems in my thesis, but my chair thought it would just muddy the waters of my argument. And he was probably right. Another fun fact: Did you know Harrison Gale wrote a novel, well, more of a novella, or novelette even? *Figures in Blue*—a strange story about an artist and the Minotaur. It was hard as heck to track down a copy of. I may be the only person, besides Gale's editor, who's ever read it. Then I ended up not even writing about it in my thesis.

Meanwhile they finished the bottle of merlot. Beth considered ordering another.

That's a bad idea, he said. We still have to walk to the hotel. Granted it's just next door, but another bottle of wine could turn the trip into a Jack London story.

The voice of reason—not always a quality I like, but this time. . . .

How about once we get home safe and sound we retire to the Livingstone's bar for an Irish coffee? For some reason this Sicilian cuisine has given me a yen for Jameson—or perhaps it's just the frigid weather.

45

That's better—much less reasonable. Also, it has the hint of an Irish wake for Elizabeth Winters.

They paid their bills and retrieved their coats. He held Beth's for her. Then they walked out into the white, white city, weirdly quiet for the heart of a metropolis. Workers had been busy clearing snow from the sidewalks but there was still a dusting of the freshly fallen that sparkled like mica in the streetlights.

At the Livingstone, they went to their rooms to drop off their coats then rendezvoused at the bar. The streets may have been desolate but the hotel lobby and bar were a refuge from the late-winter storm. People were everywhere. The space was noisy and bustling. They placed their order, two Jameson Irish coffees, with a passing (harried) waitress and looked for somewhere to sit. He was on the verge of suggesting they take their coffees to one of their rooms when a small booth in the corner opened up, near the crimson billiard tables, and they quickly seized it, almost at a run. Another couple turned away in disappointment, visibly irritated that he and Beth had gotten the booth, probably considering their rushing unseemly.

To the victors go the spoils, Beth said after their competitors receded into the crowd.

This place is wild, he said, like everyone is already a little stir crazy from the storm. Virulent cabin fever or something. In spite of the wine and the good meal he felt antsy too. He constantly felt the phantom alert of Katie texting him. He would resist checking until he couldn't. Time and again there was no message. Then he had the thought that the vibrations he kept detecting had to do with Elizabeth Winters's implanted words; they were trying to find their way out into the world. He imagined random scraps of words appearing as text messages from an unknown caller, but that caller would be his own body leaching out a phrase or two now and then, as if Elizabeth Winters's passage was decomposing and decoupling from him. The idea could be turned into a short story.

46

Beth was saying something: a lakeview but I think that's mainly wishful thinking on the part of the management.

My room has the same issue.

The close-by crash of billiard balls as someone broke a new game caught their momentary attention.

Beth took a compact from her purse and checked herself in the small mirror. Oh my, she said, I look like a woman who's traveled all day in a snowstorm. Monstrous. Excuse me, please. She took her purse and headed toward the lobby ladies room.

He picked up his cellphone, which had automatically latched onto the hotel's wi-fi, but nothing had updated for a while. Either the snow was interfering with some connection somewhere, or there were so many guests their wi-fi needs had overwhelmed the hotel's system. He switched off wi-fi and all manner of social media updates appeared, as well as emails and other alerts. No text messages, though.

A waitress brought their coffees, topped with whipped cream. He began spooning the sweet topping into his drink when a man with a blond beard and wearing a Fair Isle turtleneck stopped at his table. You're a Logos. I saw you there, right? The man had the hint of a Scandinavian accent, maybe Swedish.

Yes. The man was tall and looking at him was awkward, almost painful to his neck.

Did you take the chip?

He was confused and didn't respond right away.

Did you decline? Some Logos declined.

Oh. I'm chipped. He touched his hip.

Me too, but now I'm not too sure.

Not too sure about what? His coffee was getting cold.

The Aussie at the bar, the fellow in the red sweater—he heard that this is all a CIA plot. Your government found out some of Elizabeth Winters's followers are radicals, and the Logos project is about getting them chipped. So CIA and Homeland can track their movements. The Aussie says Elizabeth Winters agreed to

47

it because the IRS had her over a barrel—Isn't that what you Americans say?—but then the CIA took her out so she couldn't have a change of heart and, what, blow on the whistle.

Beth returned to the table.

That's quite a story, he said.

What's that? asked Beth, getting settled.

I'll enlighten you a little later.

Food for thought, said the Swede, or Finn, raising his glass of beer. Have a good evening. The Swede looked at him with a confederate's eye, as if leaving them alone so he could continue his efforts at seduction. Was he trying to seduce Beth? Or at least leaving open an invitation for her to seduce him? And was the vibe so obvious?

What was that about? Beth had freshened her makeup and brushed her hair into order.

The conspiracy theories have begun.

I think they began the moment the plane went down. A woman in the bathroom said Elizabeth Winters was spotted at the college, that she was one of the auditorium ushers, in a wig and heavily made up.

That's an amateur story compared to this guy's—or more specifically, the Aussie who allegedly told it to him at the bar.

They stirred the whipped cream into their coffees and sipped at them. The whiskey warmed his throat and chest, like swallowing a thimbleful of sunlight. It even seemed to warm the spot where the chip was inserted. He imagined it glowing beneath his clothes. Tingling slightly. The rumor that it was a government transmitter flashed across his mind. Ridiculous. The vibration and the heat were the words teeming under his skin, like harried commuters on a subway platform, commuters confined to the station. He was certain of it as he drank down more of the Irish coffee.

I wonder how many of these people are Logos, said Beth. This is good by the way. I don't think I've drunk one of these

48

in years, which is weird considering it has some of my favorite ingredients.

Maybe you've been off-kilter for a while. Out of touch with yourself, something like that.

Ain't that the truth. A lot of pretending. That's what I've been writing about, or at least the root of what I've been writing about. Now that I think about it. Are you into Eastern philosophies, meditation, reiki, that sort of thing, yoga?

No, not really. I don't know. I did a lot of soul searching, self-exploration, something like that, last summer. Now and then my reading or film-watching would intersect with some sort of Zen-based philosophy.

Interesting. How do you think Elizabeth Winters fits into that program?

I think her writing is about tearing down traditional ways of telling a story, of viewing the world—and one has to tear down the customary to see what it's made of, to understand the agenda behind it—and hopefully see a different way. I just about said a new way, but I agree with Lichtenberg, the Adorno-esque character in *Orion*: There is nothing new under the sun—

Yet the true artist must seek the new nevertheless, finished Beth. I've never articulated Elizabeth Winters like that but now that you've contextualized her in that way, I think that disruption of the customary is something that's struck a chord with me. I know I probably don't appear very avant-garde, a librarian from Madison, Wisconsin, but. . . .

Appearances can be deceiving. He noticed Beth's ring finger twitch, the antique-looking ring rolling askew, the modest stone becoming off-center. Perhaps Elizabeth Winters's death will act as a sort of catalyst to, I don't know, *vibrate* you onto the path you're meant to be on, like strings needing a certain vibration to achieve a particular note, a particular frequency.

How do you mean?

I don't know . . . I believe the world, or cosmos, whatever you want to call it, is a balance-seeking organism, and a cataclysmic event like the sudden and violent death of the author will send out shockwaves which will be felt especially profoundly by devotees of the author—and those shockwaves, those seismic shifts, will move the pieces around on the chessboard. They will change the game forever, every piece will suddenly be in a new position, will have an altered perspective—will suddenly be in an entirely new game. Like here we are, anticipating tomorrow's memorial, which is happening only because of the accident. Revelation was supposed to be a one-day thing, one and done. Or maybe it's just the Jameson talking. He took another drink.

No . . . no, it's not the Jameson. What you're saying makes perfect sense.

Unless it's just the Jameson listening too.

The Swede and the Aussie were next to their table. Elizabeth Winters has been seen at the Sportsman's Club hotel, said the Swede. A Logos staying there just texted me. A group of us are hiking over there—it's less than two kilometers. A brisk hike in the snow.

Just about a mile, said the Aussie.

A group of three women and another man were pulling on their coats and hats near the bar. Other Logos apparently.

Just a hoax, or wishful thinking, whatever you want to call it, said Beth. Surely.

One way to find out, said the Aussie, grinning. He had coal black hair and a matching beard except for two spots of white hair, almost perfectly round, on either side of his chin.

What do you think? he said to Beth, almost privately.

I'm game.

We have to get our coats. Five minutes?

We'll meet you at the door, or just outside if we get too warm. The Swede was excited about the adventure.

He knew it was ridiculous, to traverse the city's frozen sidewalks, with a temperature in the teens, because of a rumor that

50

couldn't be true. But the whiskey, chasing the merlot, encouraged the ridiculous, as did the single brief text from Katie. He almost wished he hadn't heard from her at all. Her contacting him as she did was enigmatic whereas there would've been no mystery to her silence. The message stirred up emotions and questions and hopes that had been suffocating to death beneath the ashes of their ended relationship. Now the brief breath of resurrection threatened to undo all that dying, to reawaken the hurt and confusion.

There was a round of introductions among the small troupe of Logos as they began their walk to the Sportsman's Club. Names, hometowns, and the words they had tattooed on their persons. After only a couple of blocks he discovered his recollection of names and towns was already spotty but he remembered each of their Logos: Added to his and Beth's *pupils* and *radiant* were *seems*, *here*, *these*, *Germanness*, *too*, *deliberately*, *quite*, and *the*.

The Swede, who was in fact Norwegian, but had already become Too in his mind, continued his leadership of the group and tried to keep a merry banter going, about people's backgrounds and about Elizabeth Winters and Logos. However, the air was too cold and the footing too treacherous; and soon everyone was quietly concentrating on simply making it to the hotel. Deliberately, a middle-aged fellow, was wearing dress loafers, with little tassels and probably leather soles, and he especially was struggling with the icy sidewalks and streets. In fact each transition from one to the other was particularly harrowing. Eventually Beth took Deliberately's arm to stabilize him. She pretended he was gallantly escorting her.

Before they had grown silent, the group developed a quick camaraderie. At least he felt that they had, that it was a shared sense. The words on their skin, and even more so the words beneath it, linked them in a unique way. They were squares of the same quilt, pieces of a whole. Strangely, he felt that the mystery of the whole—the fact that the pattern of the quilt could nev-

51

er be known, at least not by them—actually strengthened their bond, deepened their feeling of family.

A yellow pedestrian warning flashed on a traffic pole and was reflected in a boutique's frosty window. Too, the Swede (the Norwegian), halted the group, not wanting to risk crossing the street (E. Jackson, said the sign, partially covered in snow and frost), even though traffic was all but nonexistent. Standing still, leaning a bit into the bitter wind, he thought of Katie and her likely return to her faith. Perhaps it wasn't a matter of believing in God and heaven and hell, but belief in the bond of a shared narrative, faith in the familiar: Adam, Eve, the apple, the flood, giants and lions and the raising of the dead, walking on water, the wine, the loaves and fishes, the crucifixion, apotheosis—a crazy tale, as disjointedly postmodern as Pynchon, as hallucinatory as Burroughs, as fantastical as Borges.

Life after death. And was Elizabeth Winters not promising a kind of immortality by being a bearer of her tale? By being forever associated with her book. Something that may survive the fall and rise and fall again of civilizations.

They had crossed Adams Street and were getting close to their destination. His nose was numb with cold, his eyes watery in the ceaseless wind off the lake, only a half mile somewhere to their right.

The woman he thought of as Germanness, ironically short and dark-featured beneath a faux-fur hat, slipped and caught her balance against a traffic-light pole. It made him realize the group had an equally treacherous walk to return to the Livingstone eventually. Taking cabs back seemed in order. They had decided to walk in the first place due to the adrenaline of the adventure, almost an expeditionary feeling, and no doubt whatever alcohol they had each consumed. He fished his phone out of his coat pocket with his gloved hand. It had taken them more than thirty minutes to traverse the not-quite mile and a quarter. His mellow Jameson buzz had evaporated and he wondered

52

what the hell he was doing in the cold, chasing an obvious hoax. On some level he didn't want Beth to see him as straitlaced, stitched-up. A party pooper. What is more, it would have triggered a jealous reaction if she'd gone off in the Swede's group (the Norwegian's) while he stayed behind, warm and levelheaded and alone.

The Sportsman's Club was more ornate than the Livingstone, more extravagant by the look of its façade of brick and stone. Workers were shoveling snow and spreading salt on the sidewalk. The party entered the lobby, black and white tiles underfoot and an old-fashioned interior that seemed dim to his snow-tired eyes. Dark figures milled about or were seated on an assortment of equally darkened furniture.

Their small search party went about warming themselves, while taking off gloves, pocketing stocking-caps, loosening coats.

This way, said Germanness, apparently familiar with the hotel. She led them through the lobby and into a carpeted lounge and restaurant. Beneath her faux-fur hat her hair was blond, he had thought, but now he could see it was white—even though her face and litheness projected youth. She may have been thirty or fifty-five.

Since Elizabeth Winters's death everything seemed indefinite and unsolvable. It was as if she, alone, was the mechanism by which some sort of cosmic compass remained properly calibrated, and with her absence the gears and sprockets and gyres were slipping further and further out of sync.

The lounge area, which was intended to resemble a speakeasy of the Roaring Twenties, was crowded but not as lively as the gathering at the Livingstone. It was perhaps a more moneyed group. Patrons were mainly sitting, drinking and talking. There were no billiard tables or other amusements that encouraged people to move around. Nevertheless there was a small sea of faces and the hum of many voices speaking over each other.

With the subdued lighting and added clink of glassware, the complete tableau seemed to run together, like too-watery watercolors: no face was distinct, no voice comprehensible. In high school he had gone on a group tour of Europe, something like eleven cities in six days, and he recalled stepping off the tour bus at a market-square in Pamplona, at the peak of its business day. Exhausted from the tour's nonstop pace and still drowsy from the long ride, he found the crowd and the cacophony of Spanish-speaking voices to comprise a single organism of confusion. The locals and the tourists seemed to be all one hybrid person cloned many hundreds of times, and their voices were a multi-layered din, alien accented and more closely akin to a hive's insect hum than the marketplace drone of humans.

This sensation, in the Sportsman's lounge, was similar but on lower frequencies: less light, less color, lower volume.

Now what? said Beth, speaking mainly to the Swede, Too (the Norwegian). Too was checking his phone, specifically his Twitter feed. According to hashtag EWalive, she was seen here in the lounge . . . in the exercise room . . . getting on an elevator on the third floor. . . .

Sounds like we should split up, said the woman Quite, who was tall and lean in her REI parka of sunburst yellow.

Good idea, said Beth, stepping over to him. Chris and I will check out the exercise area.

Let's stay in touch with the Twitter hashtag, said the Aussie, Here. He and Too would check out the third-floor sighting.

Everyone paired up and headed toward their chosen search area. He and Beth decided to take the stairway to the fourth floor, where the exercise room was. Beth led the way up the carpeted steps. At each landing was a modernist-style painting, something slightly abstract and geometric in its lines, each owing a debt to Picasso or Léger. On the landing between the first and second floors was a painting of a bookshop, with customers standing or relaxing in oversized chartreuse chairs,

54

books in hand or spread open like lilies welcoming the sun, while other rectangles of books, many-colored, appeared to be ready to project themselves from the foregrounded shelves. Between the second and third floors was some sort of stargazing scene: a couple, a man and a woman, close but not touching, look nightskyward, where octagonal stars blaze here and there like queerly shaped pearls strewn across a pond of lavender ice. On the next landing: an image framed through a window, a frame within the frame, and beyond is a grayscape of old buildings, their doors and windows and steps at not-quite-correct angles, as if a quake had left them standing but only barely, and an aftershock might bring their dully colored structures tumbling down altogether, all together.

Once on the fourth floor, they followed the sign to the fitness room. Admittance required a key card but there was no need. A large window in the door offered a view of nearly the entire room, which had a single occupant: a woman in red workout clothes jogging on the treadmill. Then he noticed two little girls in the corner of the room playing with pink blocks. The woman had a long, jet-black ponytail and appeared to be of Asian descent.

Well, so much for that, he said.

Beth removed her phone from her purse and tweeted about the deadend using the hashtag. Holy cow, she said, in the last ten minutes Elizabeth Winters has been seen in two dozen places, including a Safeway in San Francisco. There's even a picture. She showed him.

Red hair, female presumably—yup, gotta be her. Never mind that we can't see her face and she looks to be about a hundred pounds heavier than any other photo I've seen of Elizabeth Winters. Isn't she vegan?

Maybe she switched to the Neanderthal diet. Neanderthal and peanutbutter diet.

Meanwhile two more tweets popped up. One from their

55

group. Beth read it: 3rd floor @sportsmanshotel nada.

Excuse us, said a woman as she and a man needed to pass by them in the hall.

Sorry, he said and stepped aside.

The pair walked past, and he and Beth looked at each other in simultaneous recognition. Beth, her back to the couple's backs, mouthed *Marian Tate*.

He nodded, watching after them.

They waited a moment then began following Marian Tate and her companion, a middle-aged fellow with thinning hair, wearing a charcoal gray business suit. They turned a corner in time to see them stop at a door. The man slid the key card from his suitcoat pocket, and they entered the room. Marian Tate and the man spoke to someone inside before the door closed completely.

Holy shit, said Beth.

Let's not let our imaginations run wild. It could be anyone in that room.

I know, but. . . . What can we do? Stake out the room all night? Pretend we're delivering room service.

We're suddenly in a Wilder-Pryor picture. It's a good thing there aren't bellboys any longer. We'd be knocking one out to steal his uniform.

Hey you two.

They turned, a little startled. It was Quite, in her sunburst parka, and Deliberately, in his impractical tasseled shoes.

So, no Elizabeth Winters on an elliptical? said Quite.

No, he said, but there's been something of a development.

They went on to describe what happened.

Holy shit, said Deliberately. Which room exactly?

They pointed it out, and Deliberately walked down the hall. They weren't sure what he was planning. He stood listening before the door, his head cocked like a German shepherd's. He was at it a minute a two before returning to the group.

56

There definitely seem to be three voices, Deliberately reported, but beyond that I can't say if they're men's or women's.

He was tempted to try his ear at the door. He'd listened to Elizabeth Winters's interviews and readings online so often he thought maybe he could recognize her voice even through a closed door. He recalled the one time he and Katie had gone away together, their first romantic get-away. Katie got food poisoning or a stomach bug hit her—whichever it was, she spent most of the evening in their hotel room's bathroom (a pricey room to celebrate their first such trip); then Katie, exhausted, turned in early and snored raucously next to him in the king-size bed, her breath tinged with vomit. Meanwhile, on the other side of the wall a couple was having the sort of night he had envisioned. It sounded like a regular Olympiad of sex, complete with a thumping headboard and the woman's unbridled shrieks of Fuck, oh fuck, yes! every time she came, which was more times than he cared to count. He thought of calling the front desk but didn't want to be a killjoy.

Down the hall the door was opening, and the four of them literally bumped into each other, Keystone Kops-like, in their spontaneous efforts to not be discovered ogling the door like deranged stalkers. When the little eruption settled, he and Quite were walking toward the room, while Beth and Deliberately strolled back in the direction of the fitness room.

It was the man, Marian Tate's companion, who emerged, now jacketless and carrying an ice bucket. He nodded to them before continuing toward the ice machine. The door shut before he and Quite were able to peek inside.

They had to maintain the ruse by walking past the alcove with the ice and vending machines. Not sure where to go they went through the stairway door and returned to the lounge area. The rest of their group was already assembled there. Information, gravid with wild theories, was exchanged. Some of the group were determined to plant themselves in the hallway until

57

the third person emerged from the room. They were anxious to return to the fourth floor, fearful that the room's mystery occupant may have slipped out in the meantime.

I think that's going too far, he said. It's a million-to-one chance the person in that room is Elizabeth Winters, and if it isn't, staking out the room is an invasion of privacy. Actually even if it is Elizabeth Winters, it's an invasion of privacy.

Chris is right, said Beth. Besides, it's been a long day, and spending the night camped in a drafty hall waiting for a door to open doesn't sound like the perfect end to it.

Too, the Norwegian, wasn't inclined to give up just yet. He and These and Quite decided to visit the fourth floor, possibly to try the direct approach of knocking on the door and engaging in conversation whoever answered it. An invasion of privacy, perhaps, but at least not a covert one.

Some of the group elected to stay at the Sportsman's Club for a drink. A significant assemblage of Logos had been discovered in the lounge, and Seems, Here, Deliberately and The wanted to join with them. The had found a small fraternity of other The's and instantly felt connected to them. In fact, his group allegiance had already shifted. He and Beth and Germanness went to the bell captain to get a cab back to the Livingstone. Soon they were in the backseat of a yellow cab driven by an African man who was still fascinated by Midwestern weather. He spoke excitedly about the late winter storm in broken English from curb to curb.

The cab pulled away, and they chatted as they prepared to enter their hotel. New hashtag, said Germanness: EWalivebust. Suddenly she slipped and went down hard on her right elbow. Christ, she said in obvious pain, immediately rolling to her left and grabbing her arm.

He and Beth helped Germanness up and into the Livingstone. The lobby had thinned out somewhat and an ottoman-like seat was open near the door. They had Germanness sit. At first she insisted she was fine but as she tried to move her arm she came to a different conclusion, wincing at the piercing pain. Shit, I bet it's broken. Skiing in college. A long time ago but I remember the pain quite clearly. Germanness's dark features looked especially haggard in the lobby's bright and unforgiving light.

Well, we have to get you to a hospital, said Beth.

I'm afraid you may be right. Shit. If you would, just get me into a cab and I can take it from there.

Don't be silly; we're going with you. Well, I'm going with you. She looked at him.

Of course, *we're* going with you. I'll tell the desk we need some assistance.

The clerk at the desk, a young woman in her twenties, called the overnight manager, a young man in his twenties who was visibly rattled to be informed that a guest had fallen just outside the hotel entrance and likely broken her arm. He had a cab called, recommended that they go to University Hospital; retrieved an icepack for Germanness's arm, and handed him a business card, on which he had quickly written his personal cell number. Call if you need anything—call me directly. In fact, let me know how Ms. Franks is doing if you would.

Hearing Germanness's last name sparked his memory, thanks to the alliteration, the double alliteration like his own name: Fran Franks she called herself when they began their trek to the Sportsman's Club. But call me Frannie, she'd said.

He handed her the icepack. Our ride will be here momentarily, Frannie. He could tell Beth noted the name too.

In the taxi en route to the hospital ER, exhaustion caught up with him and he dozed as the driver navigated the eerily deserted streets. Deserted, but far from dark. Bans of light flickered across his closed lids kaleidoscopically. Only half awake, he interpreted the roving colors as forming letters and words, but ones just beyond his comprehension, as if in a language distantly related to English. He felt that he may be close to understanding, that a gossamer touch of meaning may be filtering through the

59

gauze of semisleep—yet he was unable to grasp a more definite image, a better defined idea.

A bar of saffron light drifted across his lidded vision

\

then another of more verdant hue and at an opposing angle

/

in such rapid succession his mind interpreted them as the letter

Y.

A spot of white bounced against his optic nerve followed by neon blue which curled across his mind to form a

j.

The orange of melted sherbet serpentined as a taxi tire rolled through a rut

–

/

–

into the letter

Z.

He remained in a quasi dream state as the letter-pieces of light played upon his eyelids, sometimes forming morphemes (Mɪ Tʊ Os) but no meaning.

A white H materialized on a field of blue . . . it took him a moment to comprehend his eyes were open and he was seeing a hospital street sign in passing.

He looked at his companions. Beth was next to him, in the middle of the seat. Frannie was resting her head on Beth's shoulder while Beth stroked her uninjured arm, comforting her.

The cab pulled into a special drive for Emergency Room drop-offs and stopped at the curb.

Get her inside. I'll take care of this, he said taking his wallet from his back pocket. It took a minute or two to manage the taxi's card-reader but momentarily he was entering through the

ER's automatic doors looking for Beth and Frannie. The waiting area seemed even busier than the lobby of the Livingstone, except instead of a carnival atmosphere there was the moroseness of the ill and the injured, of the dispossessed. There was weeping and literal moaning, babies crying, children whining to their parents of their pain, dispirited adults as somber as the newly bereaved, old people, some in wheelchairs tucked away at odd angles here and there, lamenting woes that seemed unconnected to their failing health. A scene composed by Bruegel the Elder.

He found Beth and Frannie in a far corner. Beth had a clipboard and was filling out paperwork at Frannie's direction. She held the hotel's icepack on her arm. There were no open chairs so he leaned against the wall. The waiting area was an expanse of muted colors. Paint, upholstery, carpeting, all various shades of gray.

He watched Frannie as she provided answers for Beth to write on the hospital forms. Strands of Frannie's white-blond hair had fallen into her face but she was oblivious or unconcerned. Exhaustion and pain had lent her the mask of a much older woman. Her eyes were impressively bloodshot and even a touch wild looking as if she were barely restraining some antic episode.

A seat opened near them so he took it and waited. Beth delivered the forms and the clipboard to the admitting desk, then returned to wait too. No one felt the need for small talk, and he drifted into a reverie about Katie and her text message. He took out his phone and looked at it again, in part to reassure himself she'd sent it. Many things had begun to take on a dreamlike air, Katie's text most of all.

On a day autumn was transitioning into winter he and Katie decided to take a drive in the country: a rambling destinationless excursion on gray roads beneath equally leaden skies. Neither of them knew the small towns and out-of-the-way places near the university and the interstates that connected it to larger cities north and south, east and west. He'd been rereading Kerouac and itched for some time on the road, heavy on Americana with a sprinkling of adventure.

To make the experience more authentic feeling, they decided to switch off satellite radio in favor of old-fashioned AM. I didn't know AM still existed, said Katie, but soon the tuner found a crackling voice soliloquizing about soybean prices and other agricultural news.

In one small town, Elkwood, population 300, they stopped at a mom-and-pop called The Stop-Bye. They sat at a small table in the corner of the small store drinking cider and sharing a bag of kettle corn. In the picture window gray clouds rolled between inflamed maples. The Stop-Bye's lone employee was an acneed teenager who remained focused on her cellphone. He and Katie had decided to leave their phones silenced and in the glove compartment. To unplug from the world of tweets and texts and other blasé alerts for a few hours.

Elkwood was the quintessential small town. He imagined everyone knew each other, most were somehow related. He barely knew half his colleagues in the department, let alone people in the community. At the moment being a member of a tiny, tightly connected town was appealing. Then again, what if you were trapped, like a gnat in a web, in a colorless community where gossip was the main source of stimulation, where slights were committed to memory and grudges firmly held for generations, where who you were was who you were going to be, forever, eternally locked in a parabola of stunted growth, intellectually, emotionally, spiritually?

He looked at the girl behind the counter: still enthralled by her miniature-screen life.

Are you ready? asked Katie.

He drained the last drops of cider from his cup. Yup, onward and upward. Or at least outward.

In a few minutes they were rolling along the road toward the next small town. When they began their impromptu ramble, they stopped at a convenience store and bought a roadmap. He wasn't certain they still made such maps and sold them at gas stations. But they did, and Katie unfolded and spread the unwieldy thing across her lap as he drove. At first she was frustrated with its overlarge uncooperativeness and let loose some blue expletives. How did anyone get fucking anywhere before GPS? But she became oriented with their relative position on the map, and after a few miles she figured out how to fold the map so that only the rectangular section they needed was in view.

O.k. Pittsberg is about five miles ahead—not *thee* Pittsburgh of course—Pittsberg with an *e* and no *h*. It's on Pitts Creek. I assume there's a bridge.

If not, that'd be the pits.

She chortled cartoonishly.

Pittsberg turned out to be about five rundown houses and a long-abandoned gas station, something from the early part of the previous century. A rusted Sinclair sign, with its smiling green brontosaurus, still clung to a vine-ensnared pole.

A place called Elkwood is twelve miles dead ahead. Maybe it's more of a metropolis. It's at the intersection of Highway 12 and County Road 2741B. I'd love to live in apartment B at 2741 County Road 2741B. That would make me happy. To live at a palindrome.

I have a feeling there are no apartment houses on County Road 2741B—probably hardly any houses.

A girl can dream, can't she? Killjoy.

After their cider and popcorn, they got in the car and Katie studied the map. He adjusted the radio tuner trying to find some music on AM. Disembodied voices sputtered out of the speaker, some sounding as if they were being broadcast from Neptune.

This looks interesting.

What's that? he said.

63

You'll just have to see. We need to take infamous County Road 2741B—east, or left if you prefer.

They drove for a few miles on the blacktopped road, not running into a single soul. Now and then there were gravel paths leading off the road, maybe drives to farmsteads, but there were no houses in view and the fields had been harvested down to stubble.

All right. We're looking for Saint Anthony Lane. We're getting close I think. Hopefully it's marked.

The stubble suddenly gave way to a green field and a barbed-wire fence, and so near the road it seemed one could touch them, three cows—were they guernseys?—heads down cudding on grass.

The local populace, he said.

Here it is. A small white sign with black lettering, badly weathered and faded and pocked here and there by small-caliber bullets no doubt fired by farm kids blowing off steam, pointed the way to Saint Anthony's. A three which may have been an eight suggested the number of miles. He turned onto the narrow road of uneven asphalt and gravel. He hoped that the number on the sign was three.

He wanted to ask about their destination but knew Katie would keep to her vow of silence. Rocks pelted the car's undercarriage and a trail of dust rose in the rearview mirror. Barbed-wired fields, interrupted now and then by copses of ancient trees, hugged the sides of the road, which suddenly tossed up a hairpin turn, then another, then Saint Anthony's stood before them. Not a whole town but a single church.

This is it, said Katie. Pull in there, meaning a patch of white gravel in the church's yard. It's historic. It's on the map.

They got out of the car. A wind had risen and it caught Katie's long sweater as she walked. A plaque affixed to a large rock in the yard said: ST. ANTHONY'S CATHOLIC CHURCH 1893.

The church was constructed of brown brick, including the

64

steeple which rose above the severely sloped slate-tile roof. Small stained-glass windows were spaced evenly along the side of the main structure, the sanctuary (the term came back to him). The patterns within the glass were indiscernible from outside. Above the main doors black bricks had been used to form a cross pattern. At first it was difficult to detect on the weathered façade.

I wonder if it's open, said Katie, already moving toward the front steps. He easily imagined a priest in white vestments greeting congregants from the top step as the faithful filed in for mass.

Katie discovered the oaken doors, thick and sun-bleached, were unlocked, and they stepped into the dimly lit interior—they understood just how dimly lit when the door swung closed behind them. They were in the back of the sanctuary itself; there was no vestibule.

Rows of wooden pews rested in regimental order in the muted light, coming mainly from the stained-glass windows spaced evenly along both long walls. The air was heavy with wood soap and incense. Katie took off her knit cap and wandered toward the altar, flanked by statuary deep in shadow: the Virgin Mary and Jesus or Joseph . . . it was difficult to say. He, meanwhile, took in the daylit windows, which he realized depicted the stations of the cross. Nearest him was Jesus falling with the cross, which was of massive proportion and wrought of orange-brown glass. It lay upon Jesus, who appeared to cower beneath its weight. Like the cross, Jesus was sharp edges, his beard a black triangle. An oval of crimson glass, Christ's blood, has formed beneath him. From some long-ago catechism he knew this was the seventh station: Jesus falls a second time. He counted the windows along the walls, and there were seven on each side.

He walked along the wall gazing up at Christ's crucifixion in reverse order, ending with Jesus' death sentence, a window dominated by purples and yellows, from lilac to indigo, from

65

margarine to marigold.

Squeezed into a back corner of the sanctuary was a tall wooden box, like a clothing armoire, he knew was the confessional, the place where parishioners unburdened themselves regarding their misbehavior and bad thoughts, all under the fiction of anonymity. The priest would give them some prayers to pray to cleanse their conscience. He thought the confessional might be a kinky place for Katie and him to have sex. The idea may have been a fantasy remnant of the horny Catholic teenage kid version of himself—although he didn't recall the precise confessional fantasy. He and Katie were alone in the church.

When he turned to see what Katie was up to he found that she'd slid into the first pew and was leaning forward on a kneeler, praying, apparently. Her hands were folded and resting on the wooden rail, her eyes shut, and her lips perhaps moved in silent communication with the concept with which she struggled. He imagined her monologue drifting heavenward like an ethereal typescript but bumping against the high ceiling, becoming lost among the dark rafters.

111

BEAU IDEAL

The crowd stared dumbfounded as if he were speaking in a dead language: 'Give it a try,' he yelled, resorting to colloquialisms. 'What have you got to lose but your chains?'

— Eurudice

Chicago 4

AN ER NURSE CALLED FRANNIE'S NAME, AND SHE AND BETH walked through the extra-wide double doors which then swung closed behind them. He half dozed in the chair. The implanted chip seemed to vibrate beneath his skin but as he became more awake the vibrations ceased. For a time he drifted between the dream of Elizabeth Winters's words humming subcutaneously and the more wakeful sense that they were not. He recalled an electric train set from his boyhood and using the transformer to make the locomotive go faster or slower, and the sensation with the teeming chip was like that—not on or off, rather a rapid rise or fevered fall.

He checked his phone and its battery was on the brink of dying. He hadn't charged it for hours and of course didn't have a charger with him. Maybe Beth did, squirreled in her ample purse, more the size of an overnight bag. Their phones were similar. He sent a last text to Beth—phone nearly dead—and turned it off to conserve what little life he had left.

He dozed for a bit longer in the chair, his head resting against the hard wall, then came around enough to pay attention to others in the emergency room waiting area. It was just as full as when they'd arrived. A few new grimacing faces were mixed in, suggesting a steady supply of patients on this wintry night. It could be hours before Frannie was discharged—x-rays, calling in an orthopedist, setting the bone, making the cast, probably meds to pick up somewhere. He wished that he had Beth's journal of haiku which was still in her purse, now securely behind the ER's extra-large doors. There were magazines scattered here and there, and sections of newspapers in disarray. No one that he could see was reading, except perhaps a few people whose faces were bent toward their phone screens. Anyone who wasn't content to be gazing inward at their own misery was staring blankly at one of the three flat-screen TVs angled against the ceiling, carefully positioned for optimum viewing. They each displayed a different channel—the local Fox affiliate, the Weather Channel, and *The Waltons* on TV Land—all muted but with blocky closed captioning moving in black boxes over their highly defined images. He only knew *The Waltons* series by reputation. It was part of the cultural fabric, the collective conscious. In the episode that was playing a snowstorm interrupts the family's Christmas plans.

The Waltons TV was nearest so he spent a few minutes reading the dialogue and the stark scene descriptions. He thought of typing the descriptions on his phone's memo pad to create a found poem then remembered his phone was in hospice, its battery near death. There was something not right with the closed-captioning boxes. At first he thought they were simply out of sync with the action on the screen. Then he concluded it wasn't the correct captioning at all; it must've been for a different show entirely, some teen-targeted reality show. Much of the time the captioning made some sort of sense with the scene being played out on the screen, and the accidental pairing painted the scene with a patina of absurdity, rendering it more interesting than either show by itself.

All sorts of calamitous events were happening on an otherwise picturesque Christmas Eve: snow falling on Walton Mountain, a feast prepared, everything adorned in piney greenery.

A young man is sitting at a church organ, left alone in the

72

sanctuary rehearsing:

[. . . JACKSON, WHY DON'T YOU GET SOME AIR? YOU COULD WAIT ALL NIGHT. MIRANDA WILL SHOW UP IF SHE WANTS TO. SHE'LL JUST BE MAD IF YOU LOOK LIKE YOU'VE BEEN WAITING FOR HER.]

A switchboard operator speaks into an old timey microphone, a worried expression on her young face:

[. . . MIRANDA'S TEXTS ARE ALWAYS SO DUMB. NOTHING BUT STRINGS OF EMOJIS, PRAYING HANDS, PURPLE HEARTS, PILES OF POOP, EGGPLANTS—DOES SHE EVEN KNOW WHAT AN EGGPLANT IS?]

Grandpa and Grandma are in an old truck. Grandpa is driving but can't see in the snow, and the road is ice-covered. Grandma wears an expression of worry:

[. . . RENDEZVOUS AT THE HOT TUB. WEAR THE PINK SUIT OR YOUR BIRTHDAY SUIT—YOU'RE SUCH A SKANK—DUDES CAN'T BE SKANKS, ONLY BITCHES— YOU'RE THE FIRST THEN, A DUDE-SKANK. CONGRATULATIONS.]

John Boy and a black guy (on Walton Mountain?) wade into a creek to rescue a woman and her daughter. Their car slid off the road and has half broken through the ice. The car door above the water line is jammed.

[. . . SOME GUYS ARE LIKE PROS, THEY'RE LIKE PICKPOCKETS OR SOMETHING. YOU FEEL THEIR HAND SLIP UNDER YOUR TOP THEN BAM THE GIRLS ARE FREE, LIKE MAGIC. OTHER DUDES DON'T HAVE THE TALENT AT ALL. THEY NEED BOTH HANDS AND A BLOWTORCH. THEN YOU STILL HAVE TO REACH BACK AND UNDO IT—THEY'RE SO AWKWARD.]

A man's voice at the in-take desk attracted his attention. He was too far away to comprehend his words, but the tone and rhythm of his voice seemed familiar. He wore a blue parka, the kind with the hood trimmed in faux fur, except the hood was down revealing a balding head of gray hair. The man shifted his position at the desk and he recognized him in profile: Marian Tate's companion, the fellow with the ice bucket.

With that bit of comprehension the scene came more fully into focus. Marian Tate was there too, standing behind a woman in a wheelchair. The woman kept the hood of her red coat over her head, blocking a view of her face, and a blanket covered her from chin to ankle.

After another minute or two of discreet conversation with the ER receptionist, the big double doors swung open and Marian Tate wheeled the red-hooded patient in for examination. The man followed, and the doors swung shut. It seemed they had bypassed the normal in-take procedure, perhaps receiving VIP treatment. He turned on his phone. By the time everything initialized he only had four percent battery life. He typed an abbreviated message to Beth—M tate et al in er examining—and pressed send just as his phone faded completely. He didn't know if the message was sent.

He was thinking that he needed to go beyond the double-doors and see Beth and Frannie when the lights blinked once . . . twice . . . then went out altogether.

A hush came over the waiting area—the entire hospital it seemed—before the emergency lights came to life and provided some illumination; and with the dim light returned the din, but intensified. A toddler or two who'd only been moaning in discomfort before were now sobbing with anxiety. Whispered discussions were replaced by lively debate. The receptionist at the in-take desk stood and assured everyone all was well—it would no doubt be a brief interruption in power. Subtext: stay calm, be quiet. People's phone screens glowed phantasmally here and there.

He glanced at the dark gray TV screen: the Waltons and their snow-covered mountain combined with the comical closed-captioning were gone for good. He took a final look at

74

his phone's equally lifeless screen before putting it in his coat pocket. Red lights blinked above the various exits. He wondered if Beth received his message about Marian Tate, and if so what she might be able to do with the information, other than extend the antennae of her vigilance.

Suddenly he was feeling isolated, cutoff. Something significant was unfolding beyond the ER doors, and he was barred from it, banished here among the strange lights and enlivened strangers. His hip was bothering him, itching and burning where the chip had been inserted. Could there be some sort of inflammation or allergic reaction? He'd never been prone to allergies or dermal irritations, no eczema or rashes, not even acne as a teenager.

What if it was Elizabeth Winters on the other side of the emergency-room doors, and the words sensed the nearness of their author, of their mother, and they were trying to return to her? They wanted to claw their way through the confinement of his skin and fly to their source, migratory birds returning to their breeding grounds.

He rubbed his temples. It was a ridiculous thought, one which may have grown from the scattered remnants of an old *Twilight Zone* episode, buried in the black soil of his imagination.

He stopped rubbing his temples and turned to a window, where he was met by his own ghostly reflection. Sensing his isolation profoundly, he stepped close to the familiar image and pretended to be watching the snow scene beyond his transparent self, but in truth he studied this oddly lit visitant—familiar, yes, but something strange too. He blinked at the visitant's unshaven reflection and it was in the eyes where the strangeness chiefly resided. There was something penetrating about the other's pupils—and instantly he knew the meaning of the word tattooed on his shoulder: it was just these sort of pupils Elizabeth Winters had described. He was certain of it by a means he couldn't begin to explain.

75

Pupils—

He turned toward the voice with the Scandinavian accent.

I thought that was you. What are you doing here?

It took him a moment to recognize Too, who was still wearing his colorful stocking cap as he stuffed his gloves into the side pockets of his puffy jacket.

Frannie—Germanness—slipped on some ice when we got back to the hotel. Looks like she may've broken her arm.

Oh no. Too pulled off his cap and immediately began smoothing his thinning blond hair. It is an epidemic. He stepped aside and motioned toward a man in a wheelchair some distance away.

In the subdued emergency lighting he was able to discern it was Deliberately. One leg was propped up by the chair's footrest. That foot was absent its tasseled loafer.

Possibly a fractured foot, said the Norwegian.

Deliberately was filling out information on a hospital tablet. The Aussie, Here, sat in a waiting-room chair next to him. The Aussie stopped stroking his black beard and waved hello.

How long has the grid been down? asked Too.

Just a few minutes. I'm not sure. I was lost in thought or maybe half asleep.

It must have gone down just before we arrived.

You'll never guess who else is here. He paused. Marian Tate and her gentleman companion and presumably whoever else was in the hotel room. They were whisked to an examining room VIP-style. Then the power went out.

Too stared at the shut ER doors as if attempting to divine something beyond their unwelcoming façade. After a few seconds he looked at Deliberately, who was just finishing his intake information. We must reconnoiter, said Too. That is the word, yes? In *there*. He nodded at the doors.

I think so. I'm stuck out here. They only allow one visitor per patient in the ER, unless immediate family.

You must accompany our friend Deliberately then. You have

76

seen the fox. You know who you are chasing.

That casts me as a greater expert than I am, to be sure—but if Deliberately doesn't mind I'll give it a go.

Too required a moment to process the slang before taking him to Deliberately and the Aussie, and explaining the situation. Deliberately was in too much pain to care about the particulars. Deliberately was also complaining of a racing heart and shortness of breath—probably the pain's adrenaline surge—but the symptoms moved him to the top of the triage list, so momentarily they were pushing Deliberately through the ER doors; he hurried on their heels, and wheels.

The lighting was better but still deeply shadowed in the hallway paths between examination cubicles, which were basically curtains on U-shaped tracks in the ceiling. The nurse or attendant, whatever he was, in maroon scrubs, wheeled Deliberately to a bed and helped him into it, asking him a litany of questions. Other bescrubbed staff were coming and going disrobing Deliberately, taking his vital numbers, connecting him to machines, and entering information on their tablets. They seemed unaffected by the power outage. States of emergency, varying only by degree, must have been their natural habitat so the small matter of an interruption of power appeared to barely register.

He didn't want to be an uncaring friend to Deliberately, whom he barely knew, but he was eager to find Beth and to snoop around for Marian Tate's party, even though hospital policy almost certainly discouraged *snooping around* in the ER. Deliberately's cubicle quickly became crowded and chaotic—at the moment they were more concerned about a coronary episode than a broken bone.

I'm going to slip out for a second, he said. Four to six is a crowd. The beleaguered staff seemed to approve. Beyond the curtain he asked someone speeding past where there was a restroom he could use, and she motioned around the central nurse's station, to the right. On your left. The young woman in

77

light-blue scrubs had an African-sounding accent.

His request had begun as a ploy to move around the examining area, but he decided the restroom wasn't a bad idea. Walking the frenetic path, he attempted to peek, discreetly, into the various cubicles, ones which had curtains that were withdrawn a foot or two. The vibes emanating from the spaces varied from tense to traumatic, from amused to annoyed. The waves of disparate emotions seemed nearly to alter the air through which he moved, its temperature and density, even its scent, although beneath it all was the tartness of antiseptic, and fragile, if not feigned, optimism.

An impression formed. The emergency room was a living organism, but in spite of the medical (and thus biological) subtext, his sense was that the body-ER was driven by personal narratives, not the illnesses and injuries of the patients interacting with the knowledge and skillsets of the staff; rather, the stories of how the people needing attention came to be there at that given moment, combined with the stories of their friends and family who accompanied them, intersected with the stories of the doctors and nurses and other staff: life choices and career paths which brought them to the ER on this overnight shift after a late-season snowstorm, one whose narrative included an electrical blackout. All of these texts tangled and mutated—collided and replicated, reversed and revised, and at times vanished—to make the tale of his being here, now.

He found the bathroom. When he was finished, he decided to take the long way back to Deliberately's exam cubicle. He assumed the ER formed a large square or rectangle, so if he kept walking, turning at right angles, he'd manage his way back and in the process cover the entire room, surreptitiously examining each exam space, as much as he could see at least. He was pricked by a twinge of hesitation: such surveillance felt like a violation . . . a violation of privacy certainly but more than that: a violation of someone else's pain, almost an act of sadism, to

78

peer hopefully into a stranger's personal upheaval, perhaps even tragedy. To poke around in their fear and sadness, even if only for an instant.

He was reminded of Katie's objections to the Logos project. Mainly she objected because she felt Elizabeth Winters was more grandstander than serious artist, but there was also a sense of violation: an author offers up their life, their psyche, for the reader to enter if they choose—at least, an author worth their salt—but the agreement is that it's a one-way probing: the author is not allowed to probe right back, Katie had said (no, Katie had *argued*—it was an argument). He disagreed. An author—a masterful author like Elizabeth Winters—is always probing the reader, getting in their head, under their skin, colonizing their psyche and planting their flag. With Logos, Elizabeth Winters was just doing it all more overtly, more honestly even—in fact, educating us about the process.

They'd been cleaning the dinner dishes while having the argument: Katie washing, he drying. He'd become so animated in his defense he was punctuating his points by absentmindedly jabbing with a meat fork, not into Katie of course, but generally at her. For emphasis. Katie seemed repelled by his aggressiveness.

He couldn't see into all the examination cubicles, as some had curtains which were tightly drawn. It seemed likely that Marian Tate's party would try particularly hard to avoid prying eyes, especially if Elizabeth Winters, risen from the dead, was with them, if she was the one requiring medical attention. He didn't believe that Elizabeth Winters was alive, but, still, the fact he was willing to entertain the possibility, even as a remote one, suggested he thought the author could propagate such a hoax, and thus supported Katie's contention that Elizabeth Winters was more entertainer than artist, more showwoman than sage. No, he reminded himself, that issue aside, there remained the beauty of her prose, as crystalline and as piercing as icicles

79

plummeting from an unseen height. No matter whether one viewed Elizabeth Winters as risk-taking or attention-seeking, there remained the work.

Hey.

He turned. Beth was in the hall, her hand still on the curtain of the cubicle from which she'd emerged. Frannie's cubicle apparently.

I came back here with Deliberately, seems to have broken his ankle or foot in a fall.

Those loafers.

Those loafers. The Swede brought him in. The Norwegian: Too.

They took Frannie to radiology.

But that's not all. Did you get my text? My phone was dying.

No, the reception in here is terrible to the point of nonexistent.

He had Beth retreat into the exam cubicle, and he closed the curtain behind them. The lighting was subdued, even more so than the rest of the ER, with its appropriately named emergency lighting. The dimness made him recall how long it'd been since he slept. Marian Tate is here, she and two companions. The one from the room, I'm assuming, came in a wheelchair but I wasn't able to get a good look before they were spirited beyond the ER doors, very-important-person-esque.

Definitely a woman though?

Yes, well, ninety-nine percent yes. I've been skulking about since Deliberately arrived and presented an opportunity to be admitted to the sacred chamber.

Have you checked all the exam bays?

Exam bays—huh. I think of them as cubicles. I like exam bays better. Sounds more sci-fi. But, yes, pretty much—the ones I could peep into.

Ours was open just enough for me to spy you passing by. It was probably too dark for you to see in.

80

Definitely haven't been able to check them all. Maybe only half.

The lighting just then improved, and a barely audible hum returned: the power had been restored.

That's better, said Beth. Maybe we should both check on poor, ill-shod Deliberately. She batted her eyebrows conspiratorially.

Indeed. Four eyes are better than two—well, not four-eyes. How about, two sets are better than one . . . set. I'm really tired.

Please . . . gentlemen first. Beth held open the curtain.

The light was nearly dazzling in its revived brightness. It seemed to intensify all of his senses, and for the first time he noted the rubbery squeak of the rushing ER personnel through the white-white halls. The chill in the air bit at his cheeks. So, too, the antiseptic smell like lemon-infused chlorine, which had been there all along, suddenly catapulted to the foreground, the effect practically vertiginous. His impulse was to reach out and take Beth's arm, for added support, but he resisted and focused on keeping his balance until the disoriented feeling passed. Meanwhile they'd managed to reach Deliberately's bay without any sign of Martian Tate and company.

They checked on their fellow Logos, who was now attached to several machines, including a cardiac monitor. Deliberately's heartbeat spiked and receded across the screen in a regular dual rhythm. He was alone and his eyes were shut, dozing it seemed. He was in a hospital gown, and his leg and foot were stabilized by a plastic splint. He looked thin and frail beneath the ER's blanket. His round face had shed its puffiness. He seemed to have aged. They left him to his peacefulness and returned to Frannie's vacant bay, where at least they could talk. Before leaving Deliberately he had glanced at the heart monitor, and for a brief instant the rising and falling line seemed to form the word *pupils*— in a cursively blocky script. He'd blinked and the pulse returned to its normal pattern. He decided it was further evidence of his need for sleep.

81

They were almost at Frannie's bay when the door of the restroom he had used earlier opened and Marian Tate's companion emerged. He wasn't paying attention and nearly ran into them. They all paused for a moment to avoid a collision, staring back and forth. The fellow was fairly tall, six-two or -three, and likely in his fifties, with white in his dark beard and thinning hair. Bloodshot eyes peered from behind black-rimmed glasses—he looked a bit like Allen Ginsberg in middle age, but better groomed and tailored. He wore an expensive-looking gray suit and a silk tie with a diamond pattern, except every piece was disheveled and wrinkled. The snow and salt had taken their toll on his black leather wingtips. He presented the picture of a professional who'd had an unending day of travel and terrible shocks.

He felt a pang of guilt again, at disturbing the man's privacy by this more or less accidental encounter. Perhaps the disturbance of privacy had to do with how carefully he considered him, seeking more details than one would normally and naturally do in a typical chance meeting. The fellow was at a disadvantage knowing nothing of his and Beth's intentions.

They each said their excuse-mes and continued on their way. After a moment he and Beth turned to see where the man was going, but the ER was instantly bedlam, with medical staff moving every which way. One bearded nurse spoke to them as he rushed past, telling them they needed to return to their patient and stay put. We're about to be slammed, he said over his departing shoulder. In the confusion they lost sight of Marian Tate's frayed friend. They did as they were instructed and retreated into Frannie's nearby spot, still vacant.

Well, we know they're around here somewhere, said Beth, leaning against the empty bed.

Yes, somewhere in this tightly managed circus. He was thinking about seeing his Logos word on the monitor. He rubbed his shoulder and the tattoo beneath his sweater. He had the odd notion that *pupils*— had escaped his skin and was on the loose

82

in the ER, possibly trying to escape the hospital. He had an impulse to remove his sweater and t-shirt to make sure *pupils*—was still inked into his skin. He also found himself thinking of the site of Beth's *radiant* tattoo, on her hip. He sat in the only chair and wondered if it was somehow actually radiant, literally aglow just above or just below a panty line . . . he thought of tracing it in the dark with a finger . . . with . . .

You look exhausted, said Beth.

I think the whiskey and everything else have caught up with me.

You should take a siesta in Frannie's bed. In a minute I'll go check on Mr. Practical Shoes, poor guy.

You've talked me into it. I think I've started to dream on my feet.

It's no wonder. It's almost two in the morning.

How are you still going strong?

I'm a night owl. My second-wind kicked in about midnight. Even so, I wouldn't describe it as going strong, just going.

They traded places, and he stretched out on the hospital bed. It felt too good to lie down to fret over its also feeling a little awkward. There was a white blanket on the bed. He didn't get under it exactly but pulled part of it over his chest and shoulders.

At first he thought he would feel too strange to sleep, plus there was the commotion in the hall, just on the other side of the half-drawn curtain, but he slipped off within seconds. Immediately, it seemed, he dreamed of a many-roomed house, every room empty as if the occupants had moved out. The house, with its echoing wood floors, was unfamiliar. Certainly he had never lived in such a large, rambling house. He walked into a room painted light green, the color of a fancy mint at a wedding reception. He was admiring the soothing color when he noticed a dark smudge on the far wall. He went to see what it was, possibly to wipe it clean. As he came closer, the smudge took the form

83

of a word—closer still, *his* word, *pupils*— —as if written on the wall in indelible black ink. Who would do such a thing? Who would mar such a perfectly painted wall? He was still pondering the question when he walked into the adjoining room, this one painted in a glacial blue, and on the wall was another black mark—his word, he knew—larger, more noticeable. He confirmed his suspicion before moving to the next room, of saffron hue, where *pupils*— was larger still. He stepped more quickly to the next, mild lilac, larger yet. Fog, cream, sand, the palest pink . . . growing, growing . . . until his word filled a wall, the understated umber framed in the heavy black of the *p*'s' rounded heads, and brimming to the rim of the *u*'s chaliced vessel, and surrounding the *i*'s island dot like a perfect murky swamp. A sudden light distracted him from the word. Shielding his eyes, he walked toward the next room (it was a never-ending series of rooms). A figure stood in the middle of the space emitting a brilliant white light, a feminine figure, radiating a glow that enveloped him—

Beth was speaking to him. The light in the exam bay had been turned up. He squinted against its harshness and also against the pervasive disorientation. Frannie is back, Beth was saying. We need to take her to the hotel. I Ubered us a ride.

Frannie sat in a wheelchair, her arm in a cast and a sling. Her orange parka was over her legs. He thought for a second she'd broken a leg too, then recalled that was Deliberately.

What about Deliberately? he asked sitting upright and pulling himself together.

Bob's going to be awhile. Sven and Cameron are staying with him. Too and Here.

Frannie appeared to be dozing in her wheelchair.

They gave her something for the pain, said Beth, plus I'm sure she's exhausted.

You must be most of all. Sorry I checked out for a while.

It's o.k. I wrote a couple of poems, well, first drafts at least.

84

She patted her large purse. They may be awful. I'll see what they look like after some rest. The Uber chick should be here any minute.

I think the uber chick is already here. He put on his coat and got ready to push Frannie's chair.

Got her all right? asked a nurse in the hall, where Frannie was parked. The nurse looked frazzled.

Yeah, thanks. He released Frannie's brakes and got the chair rolling.

They're having a night too, said Beth quietly. Several gunshot victims came in all at once. That's what all the running around was about before. It's been pandemonium for the last couple of hours.

Holy cow. Is that how long I was out?

You clearly needed it. Looking forward to some out time myself.

I bet. What about Marian Tate et al.?

Don't know. I lost track of them. They may still be here somewhere.

A nurse at the station pressed a button and the ER doors swung open. Be safe! called the nurse. He and Beth smiled their farewells and pushed Frannie into the waiting area. Outside, he saw, it was still fully nighttime, still a couple of hours until dawn. There was of course the city's electric glow, which reflected in its artificiality off the pure white of the snow.

We're looking for a silver Camry, said Beth. I'll see if she's here. Beth walked through the sliding doors buttoning her coat and untucking her hair from her collar and scarf.

He helped Frannie into her parka as best he could, one arm in and the rest of the coat draped over her like a work-zone-orange cape.

I'm sorry to be such a bother, she said, slurring her words somewhat, she was so exhausted and medicated.

Not at all. We'll get you back to the hotel so you can get some

85

sleep—what you need more than anything right now.

I'm sure you and Radiant do too.

She's here, said Beth re-entering. She's pulled right up to the curb.

He pushed the chair outdoors and the Camry was only a few feet away.

They helped Frannie out of the chair and steadied her into the backseat. A nurse's aide was right there to retrieve the wheelchair. Beth slid in next to Frannie, and he sat in the Camry's passenger seat.

As they pulled onto the street Beth said, Thanks for driving at such an unholy time, and with the storm and all.

It's all right, said the young woman. This is my time. I'm an early riser, and there's always plenty of business believe it or not. In profile their driver looked a bit like Serena Williams, or was it Venus? He didn't really follow tennis and had trouble remembering which sister was which even though they had distinctive looks, not like sisters at all. Venus, he decided, the driver looks kind of like *Venus* Williams. An image of the planet Venus, brown and beclouded, came to him. The line of thought was a product of his drifting off. He forced himself further awake.

Beth was quiet in the backseat. He glanced over his shoulder for a second: she wasn't asleep, just watching beyond her window, at the blue-white city, which was still asleep beneath its winter-storm blanket. Maybe she was gazing inwardly as much as outwardly, dozing a little with her eyes open. In the brief moment that he watched, a bar of white-blue light ran across her face, from brow to chin, like she was being scanned by some medical device, creating an image that would exist forever somewhere. He knew he would remember the moment for a long, long time at least, if not forever. He was careful to turn his attention away before Beth found him looking.

Venus Williams came to a stop in front of the Livingstone, and they assisted Frannie into the hotel lobby.

86

I'll get her settled in, said Beth. She took a few steps with Frannie, who seemed to be practically asleep on her feet, before turning to him and saying, I know this is crazy, but I'm starving and I noticed a donut place just around the corner that seems to be open, maybe it never closes. Feel free to be sane and sensible and say no.

That sounds fine, that sounds good. I'll just wait for you here. He thought about retrieving his phone charger from his room but decided not to bother. He was too tired, and the world could wait.

Beth continued on her way to the elevators with Frannie, whose orange parka was suddenly a little hard on the eyes.

He sat in a leather club chair and wondered if it was too comfortable: perhaps Beth would find him sound asleep. He rubbed the injection site of the Logos chip. Maybe the skin itched there and tingled a bit, or maybe it was just his imagination. He recalled when he first thought Katie was acting differently toward him, toward them, toward the concept of their having a life together; and all the time he spent telling himself it was just his imagination, his paranoia. Everything was fine.

The Celtic music concert. On St. Patrick's Day they went to an event in the Student Union, Celtic Contemplation, or something like that, a quintet that played traditional Irish music. They'd purchased tickets weeks before. Katie may have been the one to bring it up in the first place: something to do on St. Patrick's besides drink, especially since it fell on a Tuesday. But the day of the concert she seemed distant, and not for the first time. He'd been trying not to notice. She taught an afternoon class and returned to the apartment later than usual. No explanation offered. He suggested grabbing a bite before the concert. Places will be packed. Besides, I had a big lunch. Katie's lack of enthusiasm for going out at all was clear, though unarticulated. At the concert, he took her hand, which had been their way since the planetarium date, but this night it seemed awkward and lit-

87

erally uncomfortable. After a few minutes Katie extracted her hand from his and placed it in the pocket of her jacket, which she hadn't removed. He tried to concentrate on the music—the Celtic musicians were accomplished (he read in the program that two of the quintet were professors emeriti of medieval music from Midwestern universities)—but he was more interested in trying to understand Katie's behavior. He calculated the days since her last period: maybe she was menstruating—though it had never affected her in this way. Wait, maybe she *wasn't* menstruating. Maybe she was late. He glanced at her profile. Her expression, like this entire episode, was an enigma.

In spite of the Celtic musicians' proficiency and good-natured enthusiasm, at intermission Katie suggested they forego the rest of the performance to get a drink at Mrs. O'Malley's, a so-so bar which on this one night each year was the local epicenter of Gaelic mayhem, green-colored beer and all. He couldn't say he'd been enjoying the concert—through no fault of the performers—so they left the Student Union and drove to the strip mall where Mrs. O'Malley's was an anchoring establishment.

As expected, Mrs. O'Malley's was in the throes of its verdant-tinted red-letter night. They parked in a space that was almost as far away from Mrs. O'Malley's as one could be and still technically be in the strip mall's lot. Inside, he and Katie squeezed into a spot at one end of the bar where a stool was miraculously open. Katie sat while he stood inelegantly wedged between her and the wall adjacent to the beleaguered men's room. Boisterous Irish music bellowed from the sound system but was barely audible above the full-throated discourse between patrons intent on something resembling conversation. He and Katie didn't bother, and he wondered if that was Katie's strategy: maneuvering him to the best place in town *not* to talk when she had to know he was positively pregnant with questions. Later it would be too late and they'd be too tired to have a meaningful dialogue about anything, or to have anything about anything,

88

meaningful or otherwise.

Ready to do something we'll both regret?

Beth was standing by his chair. It took him a second to process: the donut shop down the street. They better have old-fashions, that's all I'm sayin.

I'm more of a glazed girl myself.

Blazed, you say? He was getting up from the chair.

Glazed, glazed—with a *g*. These days at least.

In a moment they were back outside in the pristine city: even the streets had a clean white sheen because traffic had been light in the smallest hours. Daybreak was more than an hour away still, he guessed. Being disconnected from his phone and its insistent reminders of time and temperature and weather conditions—not to mention bombarding news and media updates—felt both disorienting and liberating. He'd been off the grid for a few hours, yet he felt like an electron that had broken free of its atomic bonds. His defining orbit had been replaced by an undefined course of his own making—or at least he was free to be attracted or repelled by new sets of elements intersecting his path.

At the same moment, he sensed a deepened connectedness to the other Logos in the world, the other bearers of Elizabeth Winters's words, like Beth, and Frannie, and the 751 others, concentrated in the city now but soon spreading across the country and the continents. Would physical distance diminish the sense of connection or somehow drive it even deeper, based on some law of subliminal physics akin to *Absence makes the heart grow fonder*?

The air was cold yet there was already a hint of the warming trend which would turn the white into water, winter redux into revived spring. Even as he acknowledged that he didn't want to separate from Beth, he knew it was a ridiculous attachment. She very likely had a husband back in Madison—she wore a ring, though it seemed more a family heirloom than a wedding band—maybe even children. Not to mention she lived in Madison, hours away by train or car. They would part company after the memorial, probably hug goodbye after all they'd been through, vow to stay in touch, and eventually become fond ghosts on each other's Twitter feed, their attachment to one another relegated to the hauntingly heart-shaped likes and occasional re-tweets reserved for special displays of solidarity and commitment.

Before entering the donut shop—Dough Boys, whose mascot was a caricature of a grinning First World War solider eating a donut—Beth stopped and stared into the distance. She was apparently looking at the lake, the one they could only see tiny slivers of from their hotel rooms. From here the lake was an expanse of darkness which contrasted starkly with the otherwise white world. However, it bled seamlessly into the nightsky so that one could allow one's perception to see the sky descending to the very edge of the shoreline, a sweeping monolith of black, a dark dome whose perimeter was finite and easily reachable. After a moment he noticed a red light leisurely blinking in the distance, and it may have been something on the water or in the sky. He thought of the opening chapter of *Orion* when the satellite crashes to earth, landing dead center on the fifty-yard line just as Yale is about to kick off to Army, and the 65,000 frenzied fans fall instantly silent. The scene foreshadows one of the novel's concerns: the conflict between liberal arts and the military-industrial complex, set up as a David-versus-Goliath dynamic, except that this time Goliath pummels poor David after all, one of the darkly humorous aspects of the book.

Shall we? said Beth, and he held the door for her.

They were instantly met with the sweet yeasty smell of donuts competing with the aroma of potently dark-roasted coffee. There were a half dozen souls in Dough Boys, scattered here and there, alone, one or two looking at their phones, another on a laptop. Behind the counter was a young woman in an overlarge cream sweater and a Chicago Bears stocking cap. She didn't appear to be a morning person.

Is it still too late to drink coffee, Beth said to him, or have we bypassed such considerations completely?

I think we flew right past that issue. At this point I don't think cocaine would keep me from sleeping, leave be some run-of-the-mill caffeine. Oh, for the record, I'm speaking from very limited experience.

You've rarely had caffeine before? I'd never have guessed.

They were standing before the glass display counter, which offered a cheerfully well-lighted panorama of donut heaven.

The view alone, he said, is making my blood sugar spike.

I'll have a glazed and a cup of Ethiopian, black.

He hadn't noticed that the coffees were listed by country. The Ethiopian, black too, and a buttermilk, please. It looks dunkable. That's important.

The barely awake counter girl managed the entire transaction without uttering a syllable.

They each paid for their order then took their donuts and coffees to a table near the window, from where they could see the darkened lake-sky, and its blinking crimson light.

Lordy this is good. God grant me the strength not to buy a half dozen for the road, said Beth, her eyes shut as she savored the first bite.

I have to admit it's hitting the spot. After another blissful bite, he said, What about those poems you wrote while I was down for the count? You don't have to share them. Just tell me about them, as opaquely as you like.

Beth took a sip of coffee. Well, ok, I'll definitely talk about one of them.

That's a start.

Who knows why we think of what we do, maybe because the hospital halls seemed so sterile, sterile in a bad way, and cold, but it got me thinking about my grandparents' house, a big old rambling Victorian-inspired affair—not about when they were

91

alive and that house was the site of so many wonderful memories, downright Rockwellian; I'm almost embarrassed to acknowledge my privilege. Later. Grandpa outlived Grandma by a few years, and he got rid of a few things, but when he passed—this was five, six years ago—the old house suddenly became a cluttered museum. My folks ended up hiring an auctioneer to liquidate all the stuff they didn't want, which was a lot. Sitting there in the ER I got to thinking about my final visit to the house. It was completely empty, not a single stick of furniture, not so much as a water glass in the cabinets. So my poem is about that empty space, and about loss. Each stanza is about a different room as I walk from one cold, echoing space to the next. They seem never-ending. In the poem I'm recalling what had been, but really I think it's more about what might've been.

Might've been? The Ethiopian coffee seemed to be filling a void in his soul that only could be filled by Ethiopian coffee. It was ambrosial, mystical.

I guess growing up I always imagined I'd have a big house like that, overrun with kids—my kids, nieces and nephews, neighbor kids, with a few dogs and cats and maybe an iguana or two thrown into the mix for good measure—but that's not going to happen. First of all, who can afford a big house these days, and the upkeep, besides a two-physician family? I suppose a doctor and a lawyer could scrape by.

If the doctor is a surgeon.

Right. Beth drank from her cup.

He recalled his dream of the empty house, which he must've been dreaming about the time Beth was composing her poem. In spite of the life-affirming coffee, his brain was too tired to decide if there was anything to be made of the uncanniness. He said, What else, besides the financial unlikeliness of owning a big house? I know I'm prying but I'm too tired to care.

And maybe I'm too tired to parry your interrogatories. I took a fencing class in college. I wasn't very good, but I dug the outfit.

He drank more coffee and thought of getting a refill.

Another thing is there aren't going to be lots of nieces and nephews. I only have one sibling, my sister, Kathy, and she and her husband are stopping after one. They have a little girl, Erin, a beautiful little girl, but she has significant developmental issues. They can't afford another child, especially if that one turns out to be special-needs too. They can't afford it financially or emotionally or even just physically I think. They love little Erin—she's a precious little girl—but she's a twenty-four-seven responsibility. Feeding tube, a litany of meds, physical therapy, the whole nine yards.

Wow. That's hard.

Yeah. Kathy always envisioned a big brood, too, I think. It's funny that I have to qualify it with I think. That's just the impression I always had. We never really talked about it expressly. Maybe I was projecting my own beau ideal.

Was? Sorry, still in prying mode.

Beth drank more coffee, clearly hesitating. Her cup had to be all but empty. She put it down, not releasing it. He thought of her cold fingers when they shook hands in greeting, in the lobby of the Livingstone, more hours ago than he could calculate at the moment. Yes, she said finally, everything about that picture has been shattered. Well, I suppose shattered is overly dramatic; maybe systematically dismantled, piece by piece, is a more apropos description.

I'm sorry.

Don't be. I'm starting to think that silly dream encouraged me to make some bad choices, to not be true to myself. I'm sorry. I know I'm being annoyingly cryptic.

Well, yes, cryptic, but not annoyingly. Perhaps intriguingly.

Like an emotional striptease or something. Hey that's not bad, emotional striptease. Dibs on the phrase.

It's all yours. If I use it, I'll credit accordingly.

What about you? Have you realized your beau ideal?

93

No, not completely. Thought maybe I was making progress, but it seems I was mistaken. In truth, I don't think I've been operating with some sort of perfect life in mind. It's been a more organic process—although that's likely a kinder way of characterizing it than others might.

Well, fuck others.

Her sudden declaration caught him off guard. Yes . . . fuck others. He raised his cup.

Beth raised hers, and they toasted with the last drops of their potent black brew.

O.k., she said. I suppose we should try to sleep before the sun comes up. Otherwise I'll really be in bad shape for the memorial.

Cripes. I still haven't switched my train reservation. First order of business at the hotel. Then blessed sleep. I trust.

IV

THE MASQUERADE OF PROSE

Would he dare do that: bring a dog into the opera, allow it to loose its own lament to the heavens between the strophes of lovelorn Teresa? Why not? Surely, in a work that will never be performed, all things are permitted?

— J. M. Coetzee

Chicago 3

THE STORM HAD PASSED, AND BRILLIANT DAYLIGHT STREAMED through the separation of the window curtains. A bar of yellow light fell across the pillows to his left and along his neck. He discovered it was merely bright, with no warmth whatsoever. He'd had a couple of hours of restless sleep, literally so it seemed: sleep without rest. His mind was scattered among the various pieces of the past twenty-four hours. He thought of Beth, whose life circumstances remained behind a veil, and of Katie, who had not sent a follow-up text. There was the single question, the single expression of concern, and that was their only communication in days. And what of Elizabeth Winters? When he'd reconnected to the web, he was alerted that someone had already uploaded many of the 753 words—the 753 jpgs of tattooed words—to an Elizabeth Winters fan site, pieces of the prologue to *The Isolation of Conspiracy*, but of course in no coherent order. No one knew the order, said Marian Tate, except their late author.

So among the whirlpool swirl of his thoughts was the idea of making sense of the words. No doubt a number of Elizabeth Winters devotees, or the merely curious, or the morbidly curious, had been at work on the puzzle for hours already. He imagined the years—decades—of articles and conference papers devoted to deciphering the prologue. Like Joyce's *Finnegans*

Wake, the prologue would gain a notoriety, an infamy due to its unintelligibleness. However, Joyce's opaqueness was deliberate, whereas Elizabeth Winters's was tragic.

Unless of course it was a hoax, a publicity stunt, which he apparently didn't believe, for lying there in the comfortable hotel bed he finally felt the weight of mourning, of bereavement. Unless what he felt was the loss of Katie, or the anticipation of losing his connection to Beth. Perhaps it was the grief of losing all three, a trinity of loss.

He searched online for information about Elizabeth Winterberry and Beth Winterberry. Her staff photo and micro-bio popped up at the university's library website—English humanities and user services librarian. Two haiku in online journals. Her contributor's notes were brief and repeated the same scarcity of details. One note included her Twitter name, @E_Winterberry. He clicked on the link and followed. She was identified in a photo taken at a librarians' conference, but it was a large group photo and four years old. Beth was in back and difficult to make out. That was all he could find.

He knew he should try to sleep but it seemed pointless. A shower and coffee sounded better at the moment. It wasn't quite 7:30. In the shower he noticed a touch of redness, pinkness really, around the injection site on his hip. It didn't hurt or itch, and in fact was barely noticeable even when he was looking for it. He wondered about the piece of Elizabeth Winters's novel he carried under his skin—a story he would never know. He was connected in a unique way to the other bearers of the tale: the ultimate book club but one that could have no discussion regarding the substance of the book, only vehement speculation. He realized he'd been conjuring narratives of the prologue—almost subconsciously—based on the few words he knew: his and Beth's words, and the words of his nighttime confederates who tried to find Elizabeth Winters, almost literally characters in search of an author, the surreal made real. The prologues he conjured tended to coalesce into a story about a prep school, something Pencey Prep-like: a place from which all Holden Caufields must escape, its being the natural order of things.

When he returned home, he would print out all the word images and toy with them over time. He imagined frothy debates in hotel bars about the prologue for years, with each verbal pugilist (perhaps at times actual pugilists) convinced his reconstruction was correct. He recalled other literary riddles. When he was working on his master's he took a course in medieval literature, and one of the works they studied was *Beowulf.* The Anglo-Saxonist who taught the class professed that Anglo-Saxon had practically become a lost language by the time scholars began translating *Beowulf* into modern English at the dawn of the nineteenth century. The first stabs at translation got the story mostly wrong, and it wasn't until the 1830s—after more than a quarter century of steady scholarly effort—that they felt they had an accurate understanding of the story. Even still, parts of the poem would remain a mystery forever. A century earlier the single *Beowulf* manuscript, known as Cotton Vitellius A XV, barely survived a fire, and significant chunks of the text were destroyed. Scholars had to make their best guesses to knit the narrative together, grafting in swatches of pure speculation. He thought of other manuscripts that were lost entirely: more than a hundred pieces by the enslaved poet Phillis Wheatley, scattered and forgotten in the ramshackle aftermath of the Revolutionary War; Lord Byron's scandalous memoir, to be published posthumously but was burned instead; the stories and novel in Hadley Hemingway's stolen suitcase, much to her husband's dismay; the second and third volumes of Gogol's *Dead Souls*, lost in part to their author's self-criticism and the vicissitudes of travel; and Malcolm Lowry's magnum opus, *In the Ballast to the White Sea*, destroyed in a house fire, if it existed at all.

The Isolation of Conspiracy wasn't lost, merely hidden for the time being. And the prologue wasn't lost, only its meaning, its sense, more mysterious than the substance of *Finnegans Wake*, which spawned reading societies around the world devoted to deciphering the Irish author's final tome. Would there be such passion devoted to Elizabeth Winters's final work?

As he was dressing into his jeans and a cotton shirt, he noticed that the pad of paper on the bed's side table was written on. A couple of steps closer and he saw what'd been written: pupils—. He looked about the room and of course no one was there. Could someone have slipped into his room while he was showering and written his word on the hotel pad? He supposed it was possible, but who besides Beth and a handful of people even knew his word? And what would be the point of the prank, other than to give him an unsettling feeling?

He sat on the unmade bed and picked up the pad. The word was almost certainly written with the cheap hotel pen which lay next to the pad. The handwriting looked familiar. He picked up the pen and flipped to a clean sheet in the pad. He wrote his word as naturally as he could manage. He flipped between the two words: they were virtually identical. He must've written on the pad but had no recollection of it. Writing in his sleep, something he'd never done before. As an undergrad he'd experimented briefly with Kerouac's technique of continuing the plotlines of his dreams upon waking, resulting in Kerouac's *Book of Dreams*, but all he gained was a stressful way to wake up in the morning because most of the time he didn't recall his dreams vividly enough to pick up their narrative threads. The thought that he'd written pupils— himself disturbed him more than the idea of a stranger stealing into his room to scribble it: he, in essence, was the stranger.

He reminded himself how exhausted he'd been when he and Beth returned from the donut shop. On the brief walk he began to see strange shapes on the periphery of his vision, undefined objects that closed in on him suddenly then just as suddenly disappeared. He attributed it to sleep deprivation as he walked

102

alongside Beth, who was strangely quiet. Perhaps she had finally crashed. He felt himself to be in a half-asleep, dreamy state. For a second or two he might think it was Katie at his side before recalling more lucidly where he was and with whom. In a moment the process would repeat. While walking with *Katie* he once or twice nearly reached over to take her hand.

Or did he at one point hold Beth's hand? Seated on the hotel bed, remembering, it almost seemed he had, but surely not. He would recall it with certainty if he had. He looked again at pupils— written on the pad in his own hand, apparently, even though he had no recollection of it. Being certain of anything appeared unwise. He couldn't recall undressing and crawling under the bed covers, for example.

His cellphone face flared to life to let him know he had a text. Katie? He checked. Beth: Hopefully you're sound asleep but if not you want to do breakfast? Developments.

He typed, I'm awake. Hotel bistro? When?

Immediately. Sounds good. 20?

K

He didn't need twenty minutes to slip on his Nikes. He picked up his phone and tablet and headed to the lobby for coffee and to catch the headlines before Beth arrived. In the elevator he looked at his reflection in its mirrored interior. He probably should shave before the memorial. Or maybe he would grow a beard, something he hadn't done for years. The timing seemed off since it was nearly spring, but something felt right about the not-rightness. He was feeling the rough stubble of his chin as the doors opened to the lobby.

He went directly to the bistro, where only about a half dozen tables or booths were occupied. The one where he and Beth had their Irish coffee was open so he took it, sitting on the opposite side so that he could watch for Beth.

There appeared to be one waiter working, Mario, said his name badge. He ordered a latte with an extra shot of espresso and told Mario he was expecting one more for breakfast. Mario left two menus, single laminated sheets.

He opened his tablet to check the morning news. The world no longer considered Elizabeth Winters's death significant, not with a bomb threat at the Met in New York, a school shooting in Tennessee, an airliner landing on the wrong runway at LAX, the Dow diving nearly a hundred points, a hostage situation at a market in Madrid, an assassination attempt in Syria, a tsunami with Tokyo in its sights, a power outage affecting a hundred million in India. . . .

He had to search Elizabeth Winters to locate any updated information. There was little to report. They'd released the name of the other fatality in the crash, the pilot Meredith Overturf. Wait, what? Meredith Overturf? It was the name of one of the central characters in *Orion*. He quickly read the news report. There was no commenting on the connection. The nagging fear that it was all some elaborate (and cruel) hoax began to stir again. Beth had mentioned a development. Could this be it? Evidence of a hoax?

He decided to direct his attention elsewhere on his tablet: the weather, that's always a good, utilitarian distraction. Warmer today, mid forties, but rain beginning before noon and lasting . . . basically forever. He was about to check his hometown forecast when Beth arrived. Hair pulled back, black yoga pants, zip-front sweater, red-orange, orange Nikes. She could've passed for a college student. She slid into the booth opposite him just as Mario was bringing his latte.

That smells wonderful, she said, waving some of the espresso aroma toward her face, eyes shut.

Low-fat latte, an extra shot, he said.

She opened her eyes. I'll have one too, please.

Here. He pushed the colorful, overlarge cup and saucer toward her and nodded at Mario to bring another.

Really? said Beth. You're a prince. She put her hands around the warm cup and blew on the foam froth before sipping. Oh my

God—that's exactly what the doctor ordered, Dr. Krafft. Thank you. She sipped again.

Let me guess, he said, the development is that the pilot who died in the crash was named Meredith Overturf. Pretty suspicious.

That does sound suspicious, but look up Meredith Overturf *Aviation Magazine*. She sipped, giving him a moment.

The first item that popped up was a story in *Aviation Magazine* about a private pilot and his relationship with an eccentric author. Apparently the pilot discovered he had the same name as a character in the novel *Orion* by Elizabeth Winters. He contacted her through her website, which began a correspondence then a friendship, said the article. It turned out they actually lived fairly close to one another. Meredith had flown Elizabeth Winters to some readings and events in California, Washington, Nevada and Arizona (including, most likely, her infamous reading in Sedona). The article was seven years old.

So, the pilot had the same name as the planetarium director in *Orion*. He was finished skimming.

Yup, so not as suspicious as it sounds. Weird, and tragic, but not suspicious.

They took a moment to look over the single-page menus. When Mario returned with the other latte they placed their orders.

Veggie omelet, and toss in some turkey sausage, said Beth. I need some protein—and the fruit cup.

Mario didn't bother to write down the order.

Plain omelet, he said, with a bowl of oatmeal, cinnamon and walnuts, please.

Mario nodded and left to put in their order.

So, the development?

Right. Beth adjusted her glasses, sliding them unnoticeably higher on her nose. I crashed for a couple of hours then I woke up super thirsty for a cold drink, so I tossed on some clothes and toddled down the hall to the machines for a bottle of water and some ice, and I ran into the Aussie, Here (whose real name, you'll recall, is Cameron, she adds parenthetically); he was just going to bed—they ended up admitting poor Deliberately for further observations, so he and Sven had come back to the hotel. Anyway, while they were waiting for their ride, a limousine service arrives and who should saunter out (well, saunter is my word, I don't think Cameron used such a freighted verb, she adds parenthetically), who should saunter out of the ER doors and into the back of the limo? Marian Tate and the distinguished-looking guy, but no third person. She must've been admitted to the hospital too, or she left some other way.

Interesting.

It is interesting. And that's not all, Beth said almost under her breath before taking a sip of latte.

What?

Ok, it's more weird than plain old interesting, and maybe a little creepy—or maybe nothing, just me being overtired. It did kind of freak me out for a while though.

What?

So I got my water and ice and was having a nice cold drink before going back to bed and hopefully sleeping for a couple more hours. I put my glass on the nightstand and I notice something is written on the hotel notepad—

Let me guess: the word *radiant*. Your word.

Holy crap. That's right.

Holy crap indeed. And it's your handwriting.

Yeah, maybe, I guess. I don't know. Otherwise somebody came into my room and wrote it while I was talking to the Aussie. It really weirded me out. I thought about calling hotel security. Instead I poked around my room. I even did the classic horror-movie shtick and looked behind the shower curtain. I've always wondered, What would a chick do if there really was an axe-murderer hiding behind the curtain? Pretend not to notice

106

before casually backing out of the bathroom, whistling a show tune for effect, and then making a mad dash to the door? What, are you clairvoyant?

No—it's just that I had pretty much the same experience. After taking a shower I saw that someone—me I guess—had written pupils on the hotel notepad.

No way. And you're positive it's your handwriting.

Not a hundred-percent positive but pretty darn positive. What about you? You know for sure it's your handwriting?

Like you, pretty sure. I mean, the alternative doesn't make any sense: someone knows all the Logos' words, someone who's a master forger and accomplished at B&E? And to what purpose other than to give us all the willies?

True, true, all true. I suppose we had essentially identical experiences yesterday and were more or less equally exhausted. I suppose we could've both scribbled our words on the pads while still mostly asleep, asleep enough not to recall it the next morning. It's possible. Stranger coincidences happen all the time.

You don't sound convinced, she said.

I'm working on it. It's a process.

You don't think we're being programmed by the chip, surely. Do you? Beth asked.

I don't know. No . . . and yes. Not in some science-fiction way. But clearly bearing the chip inside of us, and having had the experiences we've had so far because of it, plus the knowledge that we'll never know the story that we carry along with us, literally to our graves—all of that has in a sense been programming us, or re-programming us. But, no, I don't think there's some deliberate and mysterious revision of our brainwaves happening. I don't think. There are all kinds of stories about people behaving in weirdly similar ways—twins separated at birth and grow up apart yet both become tax accountants and marry women named Judy and drive Priuses. Or, you know, mother-daughter connections, like ESP, and they know what each other is think-

107

ing or feeling, hundreds of miles away from each other. Another thing, I had this friend in college and this guy had an older sister who was adopted, but somehow they kept it from her. I'm not sure why. Everyone in the family knew, but she didn't—then she found out by accident. She needed to get a passport or something and requested her birth certificate, something like that. She was shocked, devastated in fact, to find out she was adopted because here's the thing: my friend's mom was a Murphy or Mulligan, I forget, and the adopted sister was like the Murphyest of the Murphys. She looked like a Murphy, talked like a Murphy, laughed like a Murphy, drank like a Murphy—she was more Murphy than any other Murphy in the ginormous Murphy clan. It really freaked her out to discover she wasn't a Murphy at all. She was like Italian. She went to her doctor and said how could this be?—look at me, I'm Murphy through and through. He told her that people underestimate the influence of environment, of Nurture over Nature. She grew up eating like a Murphy, dressing like a Murphy, exercising (or not exercising) like a Murphy, talking like a Murphy. Basically her lived experience had transformed an Italian baby girl into an Irishwoman.

Wait, are you trying to tell me we're related? Were you adopted?

Ha. No—well kind of, I mean of all the billions of people in the world there's only seven-hundred and fifty or so who carry Elizabeth Winters's novel. That's a pretty close psychological connection. Even though Beth was joking, he thought someone could believe they were related, with more or less the same body type (with much of their height in their torsos), sandy hair (hers with blond highlights), green eyes (weakened from too much reading).

Beth seemed to consider it all for a moment while she sipped. I trust you were able to change your train ticket.

To five o'clock, which might be pushing it if the memorial goes past four. I may have to step out a bit early.

108

A silence blossomed like a bomb at the end of his statement: the concrete reality of their parting suddenly perched there on the table between them, as ominous as Poe's raven.

Mario brought their breakfasts.

They ate in the shadow of that silence for a while. He wondered if she sensed it too, the weight of their leave-taking. He thought she did.

Well, said Beth, we have several hours before the memorial. Normally Sundays are all about *The New York Times*, especially the *Book Review*, and more coffee than could possibly be good for me. But here we are in the big city. Surely there is plenty to do, even today. A great indie bookstore to pillage, something like that. What do you think?

A great bookstore sounds, well, great. We have one fair indie bookstore back home.

In Madison, we're in better bookstore shape than that, but I'm up for being wowed.

His tablet was next to him on the table. He entered the passcode then pushed it toward Beth. Here, it's your brainstorm. You should have the honor of choosing.

What a gentleman. She put her fork down long enough to type in a search, then returned to eating while she studied the results.

Meanwhile, the distraction afforded him the opportunity to study her. As he watched her scrolling and reading, a quizzical determination about her sculpted brow, absently replacing a strand of hair behind her ear, a life with Beth unfolded in his imagination like a game board which had been folded down to a square inside the box, now taken out and revealing the intricate mysteries of the contest, geometric section by geometric section.

Madison. A place he'd never been. It seemed a place of farm fields carefully stitched to hills, a place where cows, black and white and sonorously belled, were forever lowing. Sky and hill met in a perfect pleat, perfect enough to tear-fill Betsy Ross's patriotic eyes. The blue was blue, and the green green. Peaceful, pastoral. There were coffeehouses and bookstores, and coffee-bookhousestores, some with eclectic foci, one, perhaps, named for Bukowski, which only trafficked in aggressive poetry, another only in the cozy mystery, Murder by the Mug or Quilts & Culprits, yet another the indie store's indie store, bearing only the original owner's name, now long dead, Walcott's or Wallace's, est. 1947, a bookshop so serious readers must sign a waiver before browsing among the dangerously weighty titles, written by authors who have only coteries and cult devotees, writers who would slit their wrists, consumed with shame, if one of their works stumbled onto the *Times* bestsellers' list. Art galleries, too, of course, and local theatre (-re, not -er), and lectures at the university by prize-winning economists and mathematicians and entomologists who've discovered a new species of flea, one that only lives on a particular species of bat which only lives in a single cave deeply recessed in a mountain pass among the Andes, only rarely accessible to humans and then only at great risk. And he and Beth would attend the openings, ask provocative questions at the readings, hold hands in the lecture halls, supportively attend each other's events as their careers bloomed always-upward like sunflowers, their creativity nourished in a warm, lotus-scented bath of affection and sex through the years. And connecting them at the cosmic level was their mutual connection to Logos. Online discussions with the Logos community, one of the smallest and most select on the planet—regional get-togethers, national and international conferences, a palpable spirit of camaraderie based on the words inked into their dermis and deposited beneath it. There would be a scholarly journal, *Logos Notes* or *Elizabeth Winters Quarterly*, he and Beth would be regular contributors, or guest editors. They shared it all, births in the Logos community, professional milestones, and each devastating death throughout the years as time marched toward the release of Elizabeth Winters's final book, *The Isolation of Conspiracy.* . . .

This looks like the place: Orville's. I saw a woman at Revelation yesterday carrying an Orville's bag. I didn't know what it was. All I could think of was popcorn.

Sounds good . . . the place, not popcorn—well popcorn too.

Great. It says they open at eight on Sunday. I need to go to my room for a bit—meet you in the lobby in, say, forty-fiveish minutes?

That'll work. I trust the idea is to return before checkout.

Oh hell. I nearly forgot about that pesky detail, but, yeah, we'll have to be mindful. The timing isn't great, is it? With the memorial at two. I probably better pack while I'm at it, just in case. Better give me more like an hour then. It ain't easy being a chick.

I sympathize. An hour.

Mario brought their checks.

I got this, he said. Lunch is on you.

Fair enough. Beth drank down the last of her latte and left to return to her room.

Mario used a handheld to read his card at the table and send him a receipt.

He didn't need an hour to pack—something closer to five minutes—so he had Mario add a black coffee to the bill before paying. When it arrived he took the mug of Hawaiian to the lobby to drink in a comfortable chair while skimming through his tablet.

He felt the impulse to write, though that wasn't normally a Sunday-morning thing. It didn't feel like Sunday morning. He was off rhythm, in many ways. He wrote in the mornings, Monday through Friday, doggedly. If for some reason several days elapsed during which he didn't write (while traveling, for example), he'd become anxious and even a little irritable. The nearest sensation was being horny, the ever-present itch to have sex for

111

which there was only one relief. If he'd been celibate from writing for a few days, the urge to touch pen to paper began to burn in him. Composing creatively was a kind of meditation which kept him centered. He filtered the world through the point of his pen and the inky vortex it created on the paper. Absent the act of writing, the thoughts and feelings, the impressions, the signs and symbols began to well up in his psyche, swimming furiously but contained, seeking the only outlet that would serve their purpose.

This morning he felt especially restless. He imagined the chip beneath his skin as a kind of stimulant but instead of stimulating muscle growth or hair regeneration, it spurred language production. The Logos project had literally planted words beneath his skin, and they were growing and multiplying, doubling, tripling and quadrupling in linguistic tumult, verbs and nouns, adverbs, adjectives, gerunds and infinitives, all manner of phrases and clauses coursing through his blood seeking some weakened barrier to breach.

He drank his coffee and tried to breathe evenly. He wasn't in a position to write exactly, but he thought of something which might somewhat satisfy the craving. On his tablet, he went to the Elizabeth Winters fan site and began downloading the tattoo-word jpgs. Just fifteen for now. It was unlikely that these fifteen words went together at all—in fact, it was highly likely that they did not—but toying with them was a start. He opened a new memo on the tablet's memopad and pecked out the group of words in the same random order in which he'd downloaded their images. Then he set about trying to arrange them in an order that made some sense.

dive	hark	gold
strange	under	bones
teeth	flood	gently
unfold	toes	keep
hourly	they	rats

gold teeth gently unfold bones under rats they hourly keep
rats hourly dive under flood toes gold bones
gold bones keep strange rats under flood dive
gently gold flood rats hourly
teeth bones hark strange toes unfold gold rats
teeth bones keep gold rats
dive under strange flood hourly
dive under gold flood gently
they dive toes under rats
they unfold toes under gold rats
teeth hourly gently keep flood rats gold
under bones dive strange teeth rats
rats toes gently keep strange good teeth under flood bones
hark gold bones flood under strange dive teeth hourly

The random words took on more and more meaning the longer he toyed with them. Nouns put on the mantel of adjectives, adjectives verbs. He recalled the Zombie Poetry Project website a colleague had developed, zombie as in insects who take over a dead host's body, reanimating it into something different, some other species altogether. The way it worked, on the site, you typed a poem—any poem, a classic or an original poem you'd just written—and the zombie program chopped it into bits, re-atomized them, absorbed them into its ever-expanding database, then combined parts of your poem with bits and pieces of others' poems—to arrive at a different poem entirely, one in which you could recognize, here and there, your original, but the randomizing and juxtapositioning with other texts cast even the recognizable words and phrases into altered shades of meaning, lighting and obscuring contours of the original text—perhaps calling attention to possibilities of revision if you were working with an original poem. Or sometimes this newly created zombie poem was a thing of beauty or a thing of resonance itself, an object worth keeping in the world. If nothing else, you'd altered the database's DNA, changed it forever with the addition of your text, now in a position to migrate to others' poems, infecting them and zombiefying them with traces of you.

In his literature courses he had students do an exercise based on the theory that words have gravitational pull, a theory he attributed to his reading of Foucault, although he couldn't cite where it may have come from precisely. It could have been Derrida or Lyotard, some French poststructuralist. The great lexicographer Samuel Johnson, whose work became the basis for the OED, recognized words' mobility and in defining them placed more weight on their usage than their origin. What words meant then, in the mid-1700s, was more significant than what they meant on the tongues of the Anglo-Saxons and French-Normans. In seven centuries their meanings have moved.

He had students take a half sheet of paper and tear a hole in the center of it—the peeper he called it. Then around the peeper, like spokes radiating from a hub, students wrote six or so words that came from some other text, a text they had studied previously, or better still, one they were reading concurrently with the literature that was their primary focus. For example, when they read Shelley Jackson's story collection *The Melancholy of Anatomy*, the spoke-words may have come from an earlier experimental narrative, like Eurudice's *F/32*.

When the peeper and spoke-words were ready, he would have his students place the half sheet on any page in the primary text and see what the peeper caught, that is, what more or less circular grouping of words was revealed in the peeper. Then students would consider how one or more of the spoke-words interacted with the words and phrases caught in the peeper. How did the *pull* of the spoke-words shift the students' reading of the primary text itself?

It was mainly an exercise in disrupting regular thought patterns. Readers, especially readers who thought of themselves as

114

accomplished readers, were often satisfied with their reception and interpretation of a text after only one reading. They got it. They understood it. They saw connections. But really they had used their default decoding process and considered the text from this one familiar perspective. The peeper activity demonstrated that multiple readings could be wrung from a given chunk of text if new perspectives could be accessed. The more layers of text—the more filters—the more complex the reading. The more multifaceted the interpretations.

He received a message. Katie: Still ok?

It wasn't like her to be so staccato in her text messaging. The altered tone of her texts was the kith and kin of her altered tone face to face: the medium of texting amplified her confusion, her teetering between versions of their relationship. Only twenty-four hours ago signs of her indecisiveness about their breaking up would've been heartening. Now he didn't know what he felt.

He sensed his own wavering between possible futures, none of which was fully in his control. He didn't believe Katie was toying with him, leading him on—but if they resumed their relationship, what would be different? For that matter, what was wrong in the first place?

He heard the Norwegian's pleasantly blond baritone. Too was speaking to the young woman at the front desk, asking about the hotel's shuttle service to the airport. Apparently he wouldn't be staying for the memorial.

When Too finished his conversation and turned, he noticed him in the lobby. He strode over, smiling broadly, a lumberjack about to fell a tree.

I would guess that you and Radiant would be sleeping still.

I would guess that, too . . . Too, but it's not the case. We just had breakfast. He stood to speak with him, but still had to cast his gaze up. He considered mentioning the bookstore plan but felt protective of his outing with Beth. He didn't want anyone else tagging along. Too's itinerary would likely prevent his joining them; still, he was reluctant to advertise their plans. Instead: You must've gotten next to no sleep. How's Deliberately?

In truth I haven't been to bed. I should be at the airport to check in. I'll be sleeping soundly on my flight. They admitted Deliberately, so he is still there. His wife is flying in later today. There was something they didn't care for in the bloodwork and wanted to run other tests. They're not certain his fall was just because of the ice. There are some balance issues.

That's terrible. Hope it turns out to be nothing.

Indeed. Well, I must pack a bag and drink some coffee.

Of course. Have a safe flight.

Safe travels to you as well. Let's stay in touch—remember the hashtag, EWLogos. At Twitter I'm BigSwedeToo.

Thought you were from Norway.

I am but BigNorwegianToo doesn't have the same, what, ring?

True. It's the assonance, the internal rhyme. I'll find you.

Too clapped him on the shoulder then strode toward the elevators.

He watched him enter one just as its twin was opening. Beth emerged. He stood still as she walked toward him, buttoning her coat and adjusting her scarf and hair.

You just missed Sven, Too—he's not staying for the memorial.

That's too bad. Ready? she asked. There was something about her tone that seemed changed, not so much an added coolness but the absence of chirpy warmth, communicated in her face (sterile of expression) and the way she held herself (stiff and guarded) as much as in her voice (tone of simple statement and inquiry).

We should be able to grab a cab out front. Grabbacab. He motioned for her to lead the way, with a hint of gallantry, which would have been more exaggerated if Beth weren't suddenly dif-

116

ferent. Maybe he only imagined a change or maybe the events of the past day caught up to her. Perhaps the bookshop would restore the brightness to her mood. Already, instantly, he was thinking of the day, the moment, when Katie was no longer Katie, when the edge entered her voice: the moment she became something of a stranger. And the change occurred due to no visible stimulus. Nothing upsetting had happened between them, and as far as he could see nothing upsetting had happened to Katie at all. The shift in the tectonic plates of her emotions had taken place unseen, caused by some observation, some deduction, some decision about the world; and she wasn't inclined to let him in on it, whatever it was. In fact, when he first broached the subject, she denied anything was wrong, even that anything had changed.

Still, the iciness wouldn't completely thaw, though its edges became less sharply frigid. He sometimes would compare old messages to recent ones to reassure himself he wasn't imagining her change in tone. For one, Katie's messages had frequently been spiced with sexual innuendo before the chill.

You've been in my thoughts, thinking about what else you can enter. Lumu.

Rainy day. Meet you in bed. Lumu.

Hope your head is feeling better—I could work wonders with it.

TGIF time—F for Friday optional.

Enjoyed the shower this morning. Girls have never been so clean. Lumu.

Then one day the flirtations just stopped. Katie's messages became as mundane as market reports (soybeans up, pork futures down). For a time he tried to initiate the sexy exchanges (efforts that had always been repaid in kind), but they were met with banality or not answered at all. When he tried to discuss with her what was happening, he mentioned the altered tone of her texts (almost like exhibits in a trial). Katie insisted he was

117

imagining the change. Over time he slipped into the rhythms of this cooled iteration of their relationship. When he thought of *before*, it was like recalling another relationship, with someone else. Meanwhile even this tepid kind of coupling further crumbled. Katie wanted *something*—something that wasn't *this*, *them*—but she couldn't or wouldn't articulate it, even to herself it seemed.

The recollections played on the taxi's window glass as he and Beth sped through the city streets, still oddly quiet and white, in spite of the large raindrops that plunged from the colorless sky. Before long the snow would be washed gray by the rain; then washed away.

He looked at Beth, who was watching out her window and likely reflecting inwardly also. Reflections of a similar theme to his own? Her left hand rested on the seat. He thought of holding it. On the taxi's black seat, her hand appeared whiter than the white sleeve of her coat—not cadaverous or pallid, however: baptismally white, clean and fresh, unblemished. He wanted to touch her skin, its warmth or its coolness—it didn't matter—but he had no pretense for holding her hand, for connecting to her in so intimate a way. The ring she wore contributed to his shyness even though it broadcast a garbled message.

The taxi rolled to a stop in front of the bookstore, then they hurried to the maroon-colored awning through the big drops of rain. Inside, Orville's was heaven: café, bakery, books, books, books. A significant portion of the main floor was taken up by the café, but there was still a large space devoted to print. To their right were stacks of Sunday papers, luring them toward the café area. The fresh ink of the newspapers was intoxicating. One wanted to lay one's face on the cool sheets, cool and smooth, and huff the powerful yet friendly aroma.

First things first, said Beth. I need to keep my caffeine buzz going. As she passed the stacks of newsprint, arranged neatly in wooden bins, she let her fingers trail across *The New York Times*.

118

Tempting, my pet, but you're waiting for me at home.

It was good to see her more animated—more her old self, the Beth he'd known less than a day—yet still there was something different. He didn't follow immediately but stood watching her, thinking of her as a portrait with an unusual perspective, one captured from behind, framed by the quaint interior of Orville's. His mind eased into interpretation, analyzing the subject via the composition within the frame: Beth's white coat, among the darker elements of the store, stood out as a snowy scape, or perhaps, even, an imperceptibly inching glacier. Given the point of view, it was impossible to say if she were drifting away from or toward greater isolation. Not isolation, he revised: greater autonomy, independence—the clearly defined lines of the central figure suggested power and strength of will, not mere drift due to capricious currents.

Suddenly point-of-view reversed, and he had the dizzying sensation it was he who was moving, sliding backward. He caught himself on the nearest stack of papers, the *Tribune*. As his balance returned he noted the front-page story about Elizabeth Winters's death and the Logos project. In addition to the author's portrait there was a crowd shot of Logos waiting in the snow to enter the Dance Center. He and Beth were the focal point of the photo. He'd had no awareness their picture was taken. The photographer may have been quite a distance off using a powerful lens. However it happened, there they were, immortalized, forever linked to the event.

He wanted to tell Beth but she'd already gotten in line for her coffee. Maybe he'd point it out later. He joined her in line.

After they got their French roasts, they began drifting among the aisles and aisles of books, many of which were displayed cover facing out. He was on the lookout for unfamiliar titles and authors, yes, but he also liked to find favorites among the stacks as spotting them provided a certain reassurance about the world: it was still a place wherein lived *Ulysses* and *Finnegans Wake*,

Slaughter-House Five and *Breakfast of Champions*, *The Old Man and the Sea* and *Death in the Afternoon*, as well as all the Austens and *Jane Eyre*, *Wuthering Heights* and *Agnes Grey*. There was *Jazz*, *Song of Solomon* and the most beloved, *Beloved*. In the poetry section, *Ariel*, *Twenty Love Poems and a Song of Despair*, *Howl*, *Mountain Interval*, *The Dream of a Common Language*, *Leaves of Grass*, and *The Waste Land*. He found the Elizabeth Winters section, and it was nearly sold out. A single copy of *Orion* remained and a handful of her early collection, *Wirds of a Feather*, plus two copies of her short novel *Icarus Ascending*. As he watched, a woman picked up both copies of *Icarus* and headed toward the registers. On the one hand, he was gratified that more and more readers had suddenly discovered Elizabeth Winters, but he also felt a subtly hostile possessiveness of her and a prick of pique at the macabre audacity of those who only came to appreciate her upon her death. Elizabeth Winters's devotees were something between a coterie and a cult. Death threatened to make her conventionally popular. At least the Logos would maintain her uniqueness among American authors, among all authors.

Without thinking why, he set down his cup of coffee and reached out with both hands to touch the covers of *Orion* and *Wirds of a Feather*, which felt like completing a circuit with Elizabeth Winters's words swimming in his circulatory system, though the encrypted prose remained embedded at his hip. Still, he experienced a sensation akin to electricity flowing from *Wirds* to *Orion* through him, perhaps even recoding his DNA, turning him into something other than what he had been, something more he hoped.

He released the books, or they released him, and he moved on to further browsing with his coffee.

He turned a corner and ran into Beth, who was studying a paperback. He thought of not interrupting but she said without looking at him, William H. Gass, *Fiction and the Figures of*

Life—I think I've heard about this book. Are you familiar?

I am. I have my grad seminar on the philosophy of fiction read and respond to "The Artist and Society," one of the pieces.

The final piece. I just saw it. Beth turned to it. Really good, I guess?

I think so. "The Artist and Society" is about the purpose of art, writing as an art form, or what its purpose ought to be. Gass wrote it during the Vietnam era but, to me, it seems relevant to any time, to all times. It's universal and eternal.

Hmm. You've piqued my curiosity. Stay here for now, sweet book. Mama will probably be back.

Beth continued sipping and browsing. He wandered in a different direction. He came across a section of books grouped together because of their association with the city: novels and collections of poetry and fiction either set in the city or about the city or written by a local author. It was the store's City Celebration section. There was Harrison Gale's seminal collection, *El Is for Loss and Other Poems*, placed next to the poet who'd most inspired Gale, Carl Sandburg. Then there were the Bronzeville poets and writers, Gwendolyn Brooks prominent among them. And Richard Wright. He spied a copy of Hemingway's Nick Adams stories. He felt a restlessness he hadn't experienced for a long while but knew well: it was the restlessness to write something noteworthy, something remarkable, something great. Not simply to write, to just get words on a page competently enough rendered to find publication somewhere. Rather, to produce something special, truly powerful, even magical—something worthy of sitting here on these exalted shelves with Sandburg and Brooks and Wright and Gale, Hemingway and Cisneros. He felt the words welling in him, swimming, flailing for release into the world. Yet, it would not be a single seismic explosion of inspiration—some mythical Kerouacean Krakatoa of prose—but a sustained period of creative intensity, over months, over years if necessary. Even still, he was antsy to begin. Here, perhaps?

No, but on the train home. He would go to the dining car, where there were tables, and he would begin this great work, something about the city and Elizabeth Winters and the entanglement of lives. Would it be poetry or prose? Something that was both, and neither?

He knew no matter how great the book may be that almost no one would read it. That time was past. The Dark Ages had come again. Surely that meant, then, there would be a new Renaissance, one distant day—a day when again good writing would have worth, and great writing more worth. Perhaps whatever he wrote would survive until then. Even if not, it didn't matter: there was the writing of it, the making of the text—that was the important thing, the thing that made art worth doing, even if the painting was never shown, the symphony never celebrated, the play staged . . . the book read.

He would need something to begin his work. He scanned the bookstore and located the section of journals and pens . . . and there was Beth perusing them. Maybe she too had been inspired. He mused about this attraction he felt for Beth, if it had been something else all along: the beginning blossoming of his writing welling inside of him: this kindled passion for Beth was really a renewed urgency to create, to bring forth into the world something worthy of it. Worthier. His desire to create a life with Beth—a thought barely beyond pure fantasy—was a displaced desire to create a work of literature for the ages.

He migrated toward the journals and notepads and pens. There were journals of varying sizes, some with lined pages, most unlined. They had leather covers and cloth covers and covers of heavy, decorated boards. In some a vibrant ribbon could mark your place. There were all manner of pens: ballpoints, fountain, and calligraphy, in wood, plastic and metal. By the time he arrived at the section Beth had sauntered elsewhere. Her coat was over her arm so he couldn't say for certain if she'd selected anything to purchase. He was attracted to the leather-bound journals, but they seemed too precious (as if one would be afraid of making a mistake). He selected an unlined cloth-board journal in aqua blue and a gun-metal gray pen, a writing instrument that felt a little dangerous. He knew he could just as easily write his great work on a cheap Mead pad with a Pilot pen, as he always had, but he wanted to make a statement to himself: he wanted to mark a new commitment to his writing life. He didn't need a Katie or a Beth to be complete, to be whole: he needed a revitalized artistic aspect of his life, he needed to be devoted to something that would last beyond him.

He glanced back at the section where he'd just been, the section devoted to the city's authors and books. No one was there. In fact, there was an absence around it like a bubble. Elsewhere customers browsed, reading book jackets and pages opened to at random. There was a glossy oversized poster of James Patterson, ballcapped and pseudo-sage, above a display of his mass-produced mysteries, blatantly co-written by one of his stable of co-authors; and bookstore patrons milled there especially thickly. The hum of activity, the hum of commerce, seemed particularly electric when juxtaposed with the small section devoted to city-connected authors. Readers clambered for James Patterson, not Richard Wright; for Janet Evanovich, not Gwendolyn Brooks; for Nora Roberts, not Ernest Hemingway. For him, it wasn't just a matter of not wanting to write for popular appeal: he literally didn't know how. Producing such formulaic banality was beyond him.

Cynthia Ozick discussed the phenomenon in an old issue of *Salmagundi*. He had his seminar students read the interview sometimes. Ozick said something like, it wasn't *literary conscience* that prevented her from being popular and making scads of money. She simply didn't know how to do it. She referenced a Henry James story, "The Next Time," about a writer who wants to write a piece of junk, as she put it, but try as he might every story he created was a masterpiece.

123

He drank from his cup, the coffee finally sufficiently cooled, and gripped his journal and pen more securely as he moved toward another unpopulated part of the store, a section devoted to university and independent presses. Here were the story and poetry collections, the novels, the literary journals, the monographs, and the art books that attracted almost no one's attention. He noted the small presses' names imprinted on the books' spines: Tortoise, Twelve Winters, Woolfsword, Haymarket, Knee-Jerk, Artifice, Lake Street, Dancing Girl, Sundress, Agate, and (his instant favorite) Readerless Press (because of its brutal honesty). From this last press he perused a collection of prose poems, written and illustrated via collage by E. B. Bishop, whose arid author's note said only that she or he or they grew up in a small Midwestern town and attended the Art Institute. The unusual little book was titled *Malcontent*. The cover, rendered in shades of red, featured an unsettling image of a creature that was part bird and part human. Something about the slim book and its author just felt right. He added the prose poems to the journal and pen to purchase.

He thought about what separated Elizabeth Winters from these avant-garde authors. How had she achieved a level of notoriety, of fame even? It helped that she'd emerged at a time when there was still some interest in writing worth reading. Also, she'd always lived in metropolises where she could cultivate devoted readers, due to her writing, yes, but also her charismatic personality, and—he had to admit—her ability to promote her work. His thinking was dancing dangerously close to Katie's criticism of Elizabeth Winters. The one distinction remained: Elizabeth Winters's charisma and media savvy drew attention to her superior talent.

He came to the classic mysteries section: Conan Doyle, Agatha Christie, Raymond Chandler, Dick Francis, Dorothy Sayers, P. D. James, Dashiell Hammett. As a boy he'd liked mysteries—it was his father's genre of choice, which perhaps influenced his tastes—but as he matured he found the writing itself, divorced from the page-turning plots, was too basic: it was about providing information, clearly and succinctly, like newspaper accounts, detached entirely from artfully complex language. Every so often he would pick up a mystery, nostalgic for the comforting mood of his youthful reading, sitting on the floor of his bedroom, leaning against his bed, the rag rug beneath and the pillow behind providing just the right amount of cushion; the book, with the smell and the feel of its pages, angled just so to catch the light from his desk lamp, angled just so; meanwhile knowing his father was in *his* room, stretched on his bed, reading too, a mystery, his after-dinner pastime, his after-dinner passion.

He'd try to evoke all those feelings, but the book wouldn't hold his attention, in spite of the murder or kidnapping or jewel heist. The language itself failed to engage him. Also, the majority of the narrative was misinformation—red-herrings and misdirection—the precise opposite of a tightly structured novel, with echoing motifs and reflecting and refracting images.

In high school he discovered and devoured Kurt Vonnegut—*Slaughterhouse-Five* and *Breakfast of Champions* left their mark of course, as did *Mother Night, Galapagos* and *Jailbird*. It was Vonnegut's genre bending that most appealed to him, and the author's wit and wisdom. In college it was Kerouac and the Beats, the lyricism of *On the Road*, which transitioned into the poetry of *Mexico City Blues* and *Dr. Sax*, leading naturally to Ginsberg's *Howl*, hooking him on poetry just in time to switch his emphasis and initiate his tunneling backward into its tropes and traditions, its history and its heroes and heroines. By the time of his MFA he'd returned to the twentieth-century poets: Plath and Hughes, Heaney and Larkin, Lorca and Neruda, Nemerov and Giovanni, Gale and Wilson, Eliot, Rilke, Valéry, Bunting, Bishop and Moore.

Then there was the poetic prose of Elizabeth Winters and her determination to do something different. If there was little left to do with language and its shape, according to narrative theory, then the new ground must be transmission. How will readers' reception of a text affect their processing of it? And what if that text remains largely hidden and readers can only process the hint of it, its mere shadow on the surface? Elizabeth Winters seemed to want to take Hemingway's iceberg principle, which dominated twentieth-century literature, to a new depth in the new century. Hemingway felt the characters' stories—their motivations—should remain mostly below the surface of what appeared on the page, directing the action from the characters' hidden depths. Elizabeth Winters went further: the narrative mechanisms themselves should disappear from view, leaving only their opaque outline for the reader, leaving the processing of their faintest fragments nearly the whole of the narrative itself. In more than one interview she cited Samuel Beckett as an inspiration.

He sat in a comfortable chair—with his coffee, and his newly selected journal and pen and book of prose poems—considering it all as Elizabeth Winters's last novel seethed beneath his skin.

Meanwhile Beth continued to browse about the store. It appeared she'd collected at least two books she intended to purchase.

He turned his attention to the prose poetry book by E. B. Bishop and read the introduction in which the author attempted to clarify the murky genre of prose poetry. The very term, she or he or they said, communicated the cultural privileging of prose over poetry, evidenced by the fact that most people, even nonreaders—the aliterate—could name a few well-known novelists but the names of poets, especially still-living ones, would be much more of a challenge, especially if the names of children's poets, Dr. Seuss and Shel Silverstein, for example, were cordoned off. But, also, on its surface prose poetry appeared to be just prose. It tended to be parsed into paragraphs, if parsed at all, then separated into sentences, not stanzas and lines, the most readily visible indicators of poetry on the page. However, once one began reading, began processing, wrote the prose poet in the introduction, then the poetry would (or should) dominate the textual landscape with its telltale tropes: alliteration, assonance, repetition, caesura, onomatopoeia, internal rhyme. Prose poetry was really mainly poetry—poetry masquerading as prose.

The author asked rhetorically, Why not then simply write a poem? Because prose offers expansion opposed to ellipsis, the availability of more conspicuous connective tissue between images, and the opportunity for a hierarchy of ideas, layered in degrees of dominance as if by syntactic trowel.

Oriented chiefly as a poet, he was dubious of this final claim, but the prose poetry form attracted him and he was willing to reserve judgment.

He watched Beth on the far side of the store. She had several more books under her arm and was still perusing. Perhaps she was shopping for her library as well. A figure crossed behind Beth, and he realized it was Beth: he'd been observing a look-alike, and side by side not even with that much similarity. He attributed his confusion to his need for more sleep.

He continued gazing at the pages of the prose poetry book's introduction, but only gazing, not reading: the black letters on the off-white page, the uniformity of them, the abundance of them, all served to comfort him. A kind of textual security blanket, a true text-ile.

After a time—he couldn't say how long—Beth was standing by his chair. Ready to check out? she asked. She'd retrieved the Gass after all, and two other books, a Coetzee, *Waiting for the Barbarians*, and another that remained hidden to him.

He rose in affirmation and they stepped in line for the cash registers. It should only take a minute or two, he surmised. The checkout employees were sprightly and efficient, like Santa's elves in grownup, bookstore form. He glanced toward Orwell's front windows, and he and Beth were reflected there, their ghostly images holding their books and cups of coffee. He wondered briefly if their ghosts had the same reading tastes.

Then a woman by the newspapers said, It's you. You're Logos. Her hand was resting on the *Trib*'s front-page picture.

He realized they were standing in line in a more or less identical pose as the one depicted in the paper. Others were now staring at them, including the cash-register elves, momentarily fazed into inefficiency. You're Logos, repeated the woman, whom he realized was the one he mistook for Beth. From here, now, with so little resemblance, the mistake was difficult to fathom. The woman was considerably older for one thing, and heavier set, perhaps at best a matronly version of Beth, or grandmatronly, perhaps a glimpse of the future Beth Winterberry.

Yes, said the younger Beth—we're Logos. She patted her hip.

Interesting, said much-older Beth, time-traveling Beth, and went about her business.

The elves returned to their tasks, their sprightliness reanimated. Everyone did. Yet the previous moment remained. Their sudden celebrity lingered like a scent, or the after-image of a dazzling flash. He and Beth were separate and apart from everyone in the shop who'd been within the sphere of their recognition. Suddenly three planes of people existed: those who didn't know them at all, those who knew them now as Logos, and there was the plane wherein only he and Beth resided, the only one which felt to him normal and natural. He looked toward the window for their doppelgängers, to double the population of their sparse plane, but something had changed—the light, or the angle from which he gazed, something—and their reflected selves had disappeared, as ghosts will, to be replaced by the rainy city sidewalk beyond, where umbrella-sheltered strangers now and then hurried past.

128

V

THE ARTIST SPOKE

We are staying in the street where Shelley used
to live. I feel much better already, mentally and
physically. . . . I have been sitting out in a back
garden all day writing about Henry James and
Hawthorne. The roses are wonderful.

—T. S. Eliot

Chicago 8

HE LAY ON TOP OF THE BED COVER—THERE WAS TIME FOR A brief nap before checkout, and part of him felt like napping but his mind wouldn't cooperate and instead of sleeping he lay thinking. Beth was quiet on their return to the hotel, more withdrawn than during their cab ride to Orville's even. Maybe she was tired too, or processing their sudden notoriety as Logos. In the bookstore people gathered around them while also being kept from them, as if he and Beth had an invisible barrier between them and the other members of humanity in the store—even though they were all kindred souls within a dying subspecies: readers, lovers of books, lovers of literature (some). Now he and Beth and the other Logos were an infinitely smaller subspecies: not just bibliophiles but biblios themselves: living literature. Pieces of a text as enigmatic as the Dead Sea Scrolls, except with an assurance the text would be resurrected one day, disinterred, apotheosized. He hoped that the Logos would remain a unified family. He could see factions forming. Like at the Sportsman's hotel, where a special camaraderie developed between The and his fellow The's. Maybe all the articles would come together as a unique Logos club, all the A's, An's and The's, consciously excluding nouns, adjectives, adverbs, and conjunctions. He could imagine the contractions and their families would exchange holiday cards. The Logos with marks of punctuation, like himself (the bearer of a sleek and enviable em dash), would keep to themselves, feeling superior to the plain Jane word-tattoo Logos. Surely not. Surely he and Beth wouldn't run on different Logos rails, he with the nouns, she with the adjectives (probably)—he a member of the exalted punctuation class, she not.

Or was there something else at work in Beth's reticence, something unrelated to the Logos project? Perhaps she was feeling the same sort of prebereavement he was experiencing. Maybe it had to do with what she was returning to, a situation and a circumstance which caused her stress, which bled away her happiness.

Rain had fallen on them in large, cold drops as they left the bookstore. He felt the sidelong scrutiny of some of the store's patrons as they hailed a cab on the street, sheltering their purchases with the bags held close to their chests, like precious pets or infants even. Or religious relics. The rain continued its transformation of the city from white wonderland, a card from Currier and Ives, to colorless slush of steel and concrete, amid an alchemical return to solid reality.

Žižek's *the Real* was forming before their eyes, and perhaps it was the reconstitution of unsatisfactory reality that weighed upon them, upon Beth especially.

He looked at the digital clock on the nightstand, its numerical glow falling upon the enigmatic scrawl of *pupils—* on the hotel pad, and there were forty minutes before checkout. He'd shut the drapes in hopes of getting some sleep but it was a futile effort. A thin strip of gray light marked where the drapery panels didn't quite meet. His mind was wandering among abstractions, and he thought of the strip as a demarcation between phases of reality, and each of the two dark panels on either side were the *before* and *after* of the demarcated event: the line of gray light was the moment he met Katie at a department meeting, the panel on the left was his existence before as a single man focused on establishing an academic life, as a single man who felt incomplete; the right was all that came after, the hoping, the wishing, the stargazing, the poetry, the planetarium, the laughing, the loving, the road-tripping, the church, the change, the stress, the uncertainty | the moment he discovered Elizabeth Winters, the enthrallment to her prose, s/he, Orion, Wirds, Icarus, Body Cheque, Logos, everything in print, before had been directionless, Medieval verse, Shakespeare, the modernists and midcentury poets, Wilson and Gale, Ginsberg, Burroughs, Kerouac, Plath, Hughes and Heaney, Eliot and Bunting | the moment pupils— was forever etched into his skin, prior loose affiliations, opaqueness, senses of belonging with little purpose, weak fidelity to cause, but after connection, community, collaboration, conspiracy to a literary enterprise, contentment even in the contours of his crumbling relationship with Katie | a sense of sympatico since meeting Beth, a kindling of a belief in kindred spirits (and therefore, logically, a kindling of a belief in souls), an ease of company where before there had been anxiety, psychic turmoil, tension—traces of turmoil and tension had begun to tendril their way in with Beth's sudden reticence, the dampening of her soul's radiance—so would that always be the way of trying to connect, fleeting satisfaction followed by entropic collapse, soon and suddenly | before there'd been a private identity, a quiet awareness to the typical number of acquaintances, friends and family, professional connections, colleagues, students, and his scant persona in print, a handful of editors and a nearly equal number of readers, now, though, there was some other emerging identity, some more public person recognized by strangers, considered woven within some context beyond himself.

He rolled over turning his back to the drapes and the bar of gray light. He thought about how much time and emotional energy he'd invested in trying to figure out various female partners (or potential partners)—attempting to peer beyond the veil

135

of their outward gestures, to audit their words and actions and expressions to arrive at some accounting of their feelings, their wishes, their desires. In retrospect it appeared a foolish errand: there was no way to divine what lay beneath the surface. He suspected that much of the time they themselves didn't know their own heart. He barely had a greasy grasp of his own.

He checked his phone, which was on silent so he could rest. Neither Beth nor Katie had contacted him, but it was time to vacate his room. He brushed his teeth, placed the damp brush in a baggie, and packed it away. He'd found space for the book and the journal he'd bought at Orville's but it was tight. He thought: Traveling lightly requires packing tightly. At first he rather liked the construction, then decided it was more of a jingle than a line of poetry.

It was still two hours until the memorial for Elizabeth Winters. He took a last look around the room, checking drawers he knew he hadn't used, even perusing the shower. He gazed at the tiny patch of lake he could see from his window, now streaked with rain.

In the lobby he waited in line for a few minutes behind others who were checking out. He furtively glanced here and there for Beth: she was nowhere.

He thought visiting an art museum would be a worthwhile way to use a couple of hours. The Art Institute was too obvious, and it would likely be crowded. An alternative was the Museum of Contemporary Art—he searched on his phone while waiting in line. It appealed to him. He was feeling new. He wanted to create the new. The sentiment of Adorno came to him, a sentiment that he'd taken to heart and still truly believed: In art, there is nothing new under the sun, but the true artist must aim for the new nevertheless.

Outside a row of taxis waited in the rain; it was a prime time for people to be leaving the hotel, most bound for the airport or the train station. He slushed through the sidewalk to a classic

136

yellow cab, scooted into the backseat with his stuffed backpack and told the driver the Museum of Contemporary Art, on Chicago. It was a brief drive, mainly along the lake, which was leaden and inhospitable beyond the horizon, like the sea. It seemed ages ago that he'd shared a cab with Beth and Frannie returning from the hospital—even the trip to the bookstore had the feel of another time.

As the cab approached the curb in front of the museum an installation came into view: a large purple egg (two or three times taller than a person—an umbrellaed person conveniently walking past revealed) with the words THE MATERNAL in metallic gold angled along its wet surface. He assumed the piece was announcing a featured exhibit.

He paid the cabby then hurried past the egg up the museum's steps to the front doors, where a large hashtagged phrase had been professionally inscribed on a banner: #makeitnew—Ezra Pound's modernist mantra. He recognized the homophonic irony (or was it the appropriateness?) of the pound sign being the hashtag, an old symbol repurposed in the digital age.

He purchased his admission and checked his backpack and coat. The young woman at the desk, who was wearing colorfully ornate glasses, handed him a program and a device for his self-guided tour. *The Maternal* was indeed the featured exhibit in the second-floor gallery. There were other exhibits elsewhere in the museum. If he had time, maybe he would check out those as well, or visit the gift shop.

He took the stairs and discovered the stairwell itself was an artfully designed space of swirling cyclonic curves. Looking up, through the eye of the cyclone, was disorienting and he gripped the metal banister securely as he climbed. He reached the second-floor landing and entered the gallery.

The first piece in the exhibit was a free-standing panel twenty or thirty feet long, perhaps constructed of layers of glass, some of which were painted or imprinted with images of nude, preg-

137

nant women of various ethnicities. As one moved along the panel, one's image mingled with the images of pregnant women, effecting distorted representations of the viewer as female and expecting. At the end of the panel was a plaque with the title and artist: *Herspective* Susanna Moshirfatemi. He passed the tour device across the red-light scanner then held it to his ear to find out more about the installation and its artist, an Iranian-American architect. The tour's female voice spoke about the artwork briefly before a recording of the artist: So much of the world's problems are rooted in single perspective. People view complex issues through a single, narrow lens. We must strive to see via many perspectives, to project ourselves into others' circumstances.

The recording ended and he went farther into the gallery. To his left was a series of panels in a circular formation, suspended on nearly invisible wire from the ceiling. Viewed from outside they were blankly white but space between the panels invited one to enter the circle. The interior sides of the panels were of various colors—mint green, glacial blue, mild lilac, frozen fog, palest pink—and on each a word was painted in large, beautifully scripted gold letters: bitch, whore, cunt, slut, tramp. And a single letter was crudely painted in black on each panel: W, O, M, A, N. The placard with title and artist was adhered to the floor at the center of the circle: *Gilt* Helen Pirski. He passed the tour device over the scanner at his feet. The voice discussed the piece's symbolism in terms of its shape and color choices (each shade was inspired by a well-known king's throne-room). The artist spoke: I was thinking about the marriage of language and visual elements but especially about what the word *marriage* means in that context. The language and the visual affect each other, yes, but one must dominate—there cannot be perfect harmony. It's not how the cosmos operates. There are always masters and pupils—with the latter ultimately becoming and usurping the former.

138

The utterance of his word both startled and absorbed him further into contemplation of the art's meaning. He exited the circular installation in this conflicted state of alertness and introspection, hyper attentive to his own musings. As such, he barely prevented himself from running headlong into the person outside the work of art, yet didn't process the identity of the person until she spoke to him:

Chris.

Hi. Sorry. I was lost in the art.

It must be captivating, said Beth.

A sense of betrayal surrounded them like a net, as charged with meaning as any art object, a piece imbued with enigma. Who had betrayed whom? And why? Neither knew, it seemed. He didn't.

It's a provocative exhibition, she said.

Yes—it appears to be. I mean, I've only just arrived.

I always go through exhibits backward or in random order. Otherwise I feel like the gallery is manipulating me, encouraging me to see the art in a particular way, a preordained interpretation.

A good point. I suppose I feel there was a masterplan, one whose agenda was benign, and I feel obliged to respect that design. In truth I haven't really dissected my thoughts on such things. In my poems I place the stanzas in a particular order and assume readers will follow that design. I guess they don't have to. They can read them in whatever order they like, or not at all, which is probably the likeliest scenario.

That's a good point. Now I'm curious what the gallery designer's masterplan may've been, but I can't un-experience the pieces I've already taken in. Control-z my way back to entering the exhibit.

Indeed. Experiencing the exhibition for the first time is a one-way ticket. He stepped aside and raised his hand like a welcoming host. Please, step this way to experience *Gilt* (that's *gilt*, without the *u*).

Beth stepped inside the installation. He didn't follow. It seemed a piece meant to be experienced one observer at a time. He moved ahead in the exhibit. The works became more conventional, paintings and sculptures, and some found art, all on a small scale. Everything was interesting but he had difficulty engaging them fully. Part of his mind remained on the fact Beth occupied the gallery space too. As he went from piece to piece and cornered around partitions his eyes were only partly on the art; he involuntarily watched for Beth. Now on the opposite side of the gallery, he semi-watched her take in a final work of art—large nesting dolls which instead of nesting hung from the ceiling, one above the next level below—then Beth exited the gallery, without appearing to look for him. He felt a small cut of hurt at her ambivalence. Then a small cut of self-admonishment for caring.

He remained for a time among *The Maternal* artworks, listening to a few more recorded bits, before deciding to leave. It was still too early to go to the memorial. He could easily find a coffee place and read for a while. On his way out of the gallery he nodded to a woman who'd brought her two young daughters, presumably, to the exhibit. The little girls were having fun with their reflections in the *Herspective* installation.

Downstairs, he headed toward the ticket counter to retrieve his backpack and coat, but he'd only taken a few steps when Beth spoke his name. She was seated on a bench against the wall.

There's another exhibit I want to check out briefly. Game? she asked, getting up from the bench.

Sure.

It's the *Islamophilia* exhibit. She began leading the way along the main floor. Sounds like it might be right up our alley—your alley in particular. Did you read about it?

No, but I'm intrigued.

They stopped before a room where an easel displayed a large

140

placard: ISLAMOPHILIA: REFLECTIONS ON ILLUMINATED MAN-USCRIPTS FROM IRAN, IRAQ AND SYRIA. According to the small print, the books were on loan from a museum in Lisbon.

Seems like an odd exhibit for a museum of contemporary art, he said, but you're right: it does sound like us.

They entered the space.

It was a fairly small room, at least compared to the whole gallery devoted to *The Maternal*. Along the walls were glass cases which contained medieval books from Middle Eastern countries, some shut to show the art on their covers, others opened to a page with especially ornate illumination. What made the exhibit contemporary was that local Muslim artists had contributed paintings inspired by each of the books, Beth read aloud from her program. The ekphrastic pieces were displayed above the glass cases.

He and Beth separated somewhat to take in the art. They were the only patrons in the room.

The first book he examined was from the fourteenth century, Iran (Persia). It was open to a full-page illustration of a courtyard scene. Along one side of the courtyard are three trees, date trees it would seem. A young woman, veiled and wearing all white, is presumably picking the dates and placing them in a basket at her feet, which are bare. On the opposing side is a bearded man, seated on a carpet on the ground attempting to read a book. The carpet is yellow. The man wears light blue. The book is turquoise green. He seems to be only attempting to read because his gaze appears fixed on the woman gathering dates. There is a small dog, nutmeg-brown, in the courtyard too.

Above the glass case was a vertical painting whose main color is turquoise green. On the field of green are two hands extending from opposite sides. One hand appears male, dark-skinned, almost black; the other is feminine, smaller, light-skinned, nearly white. The fingertips are close to touching but not quite. The blue-green color is vivid in the space between. The painting was

141

titled *Mano a Mano*, by Yusuf C. Hassan.

He held the museum's device up to the scanner and the artist spoke: It is an ancient narrative, more than ancient, prehistoric no doubt, replicated a trillion times: boy meets girl, boy loses girl—will boy get girl back? But it's linked to myriad other binaries: East meets West, old meets young, sacred meets profane, faith meets reason, dark meets light, high meets low, life meets death. I suspect our fascination with the narrative is far more than hormonal, far more than simple biological chemistry, far more than a drive to perpetuate the species. It is the universal yearning, to draw the opposite into correspondence, into conflict.

He moved on to the next piece, and the next, not bothering to listen to all the artists' statements, usually just taking in the art on its own terms. At one point he watched Beth observing a piece, listening to the artist. She appeared fully absorbed as she considered its depths of meaning, its play of colors and images—or perhaps her mind was elsewhere, thrown backward or forward in time and place by the art, stolen from the present moment like a piece lifted by the stickiest-fingered of thieves.

There were fourteen sets of books and their inspired paintings—so browsing more than studying they were finished in little time.

Interesting, said Beth as they were leaving the space. I'd have to spend a lot more time to really take it all in.

I always feel that way when I leave a museum or art gallery. I like to think I've taken more in than I realize, that the stuff has quietly colonized my psyche and set up shop there. They were in the main hall heading to the reception desk. Maybe it's just wishful thinking.

Even if it is that's o.k. I wish it too.

They waited at the desk while the young woman in the eye-catching eyewear retrieved their things.

I thought about getting some coffee on the way to the me-

142

morial, he said.

Way ahead of you. There's a place a few blocks from the auditorium. Already googled it. She held up her phone. It's my turn to buy.

The young woman gave Beth her overnight bag and rolled out her suitcase. She paused as she took in him and Beth together. She recognized them from their *Tribune* photo, not him by himself, and not her, but side by side their identity as Logos was manifest. Who could say how far that photo had traveled on the waves of the web.

I'll call for a ride, said Beth as she went back toward the bench.

Thanks, he said, taking his pack. The young woman's tattoo sleeves poked intricately from beneath the sleeves of her sweater. He wondered if she was thoroughly inked, fully illustrated, fully illuminated from neck to toe.

It was still raining so he and Beth waited inside for their driver but only for a minute or two. From inside the glass doors they watched a red Fusion come to a stop at the curb, just beyond the purple egg and just as Beth received a text. Our chariot, she said, and they went out into the rain.

Beth had an umbrella but it presented a problem along with her bag and purse (nearly as large as an overnight bag) and her suitcase. He took the handle of the suitcase so that she could more easily open the umbrella. The umbrella was red with large white polka dots; it seemed strangely and inappropriately festive.

Before they reached the car, Beth stopped and turned to him. They were somewhat sheltered by the purple egg installation. She said, Look, I'm sorry I ditched you at the hotel. I shouldn't have. It was wrong. She was looking at him through the rain that dripped from the edge of her umbrella but almost seemed to be speaking to herself, giving voice to an internal admission, a confession.

It's o.k. Rain ran cold down his neck.

No it's not. I felt myself getting attached and it scared me. I felt like an idiot for getting attached to you. . . .

I understand, I really do. He thought of what to say, of what he wanted to say, settled for: I truly do.

Elizabeth? The driver had lowered the passenger window and was calling to them, thinking they were confused. Being correct.

Yes, said Beth. Come on. You're getting soaked.

The driver popped the trunk from inside, and he waved her to stay where she was, dry in the driver's seat. He put Beth's luggage in the trunk then scooted in next to her in the back of the Fusion.

The driver verified they were going to O'Byrn's as she pulled away from the curb.

We have just enough time for the city's best coffee before the memorial, said Beth

One can't argue with the city's best. His hair and face were wet from the rain.

After a moment she said: What did you think of the *Maternal* exhibition?

I know it's pedestrian to call it interesting but it was. I don't know that I found anything especially inspiring. Perhaps I wasn't in the proper frame of mind for the show. What about you?

Same. I felt a lot of pressure to feel something, besides pressure. I was engaged intellectually but not so much emotionally. Perhaps I'm all wrung out emotionally. Maybe I'll feel something from the art later, after it sinks in and my emotional well refills.

I feel an urge to write, he said. More than that: a yearning to write, to write something great, something meaningful. I'm sure that was impacting my appreciation of the show, distracting me.

That's a lot of pressure too. Any sense what your magnum opus will be about?

Only a sense. He considered elaborating but too much time

144

passed so instead he set back and absorbed the sights and sounds of the city.

They'd been stationary for a couple of minutes when the driver said, I'm not sure I'm going to be able to get you any closer than this.

They were stopped because of a traffic jam, not just a red light.

It's backed up for blocks. Must be a big to-do at the university. Too early in the year for graduation.

Holy cow, said Beth. Because of the memorial, you think?

Maybe. Must be.

At least the rain has let up, said the driver. She slowed the speed of her wipers.

I guess we'll have to hoof it, he said.

Just another exciting chapter in Elizabeth Winters's book.

The driver pushed the trunk release as they slid out. He removed Beth's suitcase and set it on the sidewalk. He took up her overnight bag and shouldered it, its strap overlapping one of his backpack straps.

She extended the suitcase's handle. Unto the breach.

Foot traffic on the sidewalk wasn't as snarled as the street traffic, but it was heavily congested, similar to a crowded street festival, but with a subdued vibe. There was an energy but it was the inherent energy of a mass of humanity coming together, regardless of its purpose or impetus.

This is all due to Elizabeth Winters? It's hard to believe. Beth was rolling her suitcase alongside her, rather than pulling it, causing them to make a wider wake as they maneuvered through the throng.

She never had this sort of popularity in life, unless I've been mistaken all these years.

I don't think you were mistaken, unless I was too.

The rain had transformed the snow to slush, and the foot traffic had mostly cleared the sidewalk, except for occasional puddles of gray slop. Beth tried to avoid them with her rolling suitcase. The dynamics of the crowd sometimes made avoidance impossible, however, and the case's wheels would skid or slog in the mushy slush. Beth would have to exert extra force to keep the suitcase at her side moving along.

Meanwhile, he watched for familiar faces, other Logos and especially their companions from the previous night. Everyone appeared a total stranger, hunched and wet-shouldered, and oddly quiet as they moved along alone in the crowd. He thought of Toni, the protagonist in Elizabeth Winters's story "s/he," when she tries to fit into a party but feels helplessly alone in the raucous crowd, partygoers shouting conversation at one another above the deafening beat of the music, or moving to it in a tribal version of teenage dance.

He also recalled the St. Patrick's Day date with Katie in Mrs. O'Malley's claustrophobically crowded space, and how he felt awkwardly alone that night too, among the shouting strangers and Katie, suddenly like a stranger herself, retreated into an impenetrable zone she'd constructed, impenetrable especially to him.

Now, he didn't feel alone in this frenetic crowd thanks to Beth's presence. Yet he experienced a kind of pre-aloneness, pregrief at their soon-to-be separation. He'd tried to intellectualize himself beyond it. He'd tried to articulate the absurdity of the situation: the absurdity of falling in love with her, of having fallen in love at all in the space of only a few hours.

He hoisted Beth's bag higher on his shoulder and took the opportunity to glance at her in profile, half hoping she would suddenly appear as someone who didn't evoke this maelstrom of emotions, this turmoil of the heart. She did.

They came to the coffee shop which had been their objective and nearly didn't realize it. There were so many people loitering on the walk in front of O'Byrn's they obscured its name.

Should we bother? asked Beth.

146

Let's take a look. Maybe it's not as bad inside.

They managed their way through the coffee crowd—excuse me, pardon us. There was nowhere to sit but the line to order wasn't terrible. They exchanged glances then took up a spot in line. It was warm inside the shop, with so many customers packed together. Beth removed her coat and folded it over her suitcase. Her Logos pass, in a kind of periwinkle blue, hung around her neck like an amulet.

Voices babbled all around, mostly indecipherable except for the odd snippet, mostly meaningless. Their turn to order came. Three bearded and harried baristas behind the counter ground and pressed and poured and streamed as if monks on a holy mission. They ordered café Americanos, Beth paid, and they waited as best they could off to the side.

A man in a shabby black trench coat came up to the counter and picked up a napkin from a disheveled stack. He paused. You're one of those. He nodded toward Beth's pass. Logos. He looked at him but his pass was hidden beneath his coat. So what's your take? Murder-suicide, double-suicide, or a terrible coincidence?

He and Beth looked at each other.

Where've you two been? They found a note. The man turned away without further explanation.

Their Americanos were ready. They made their way outdoors. He held Beth's cup while she put her coat back on without buttoning it.

What was that?

Let's find out. She took her phone from her purse. There are alerts.

He wanted to check his phone too but was manacled by the cups of coffee.

Beth was silent for a few moments as she skimmed the bits of news. Wow. Apparently a note was found in the pilot's locker, Meredith Overturf, and it reads like a suicide note. I guess an-

147

other pilot found it and tweeted. He said he was going to post a picture of it but so far hasn't apparently.

Maybe a sudden pang of decency.

Or the authorities.

What did the guy mean suicide-suicide?

Beth was still skimming. I guess there's a rumor that Elizabeth Winters was sick—people are speculating the plane crash was a suicide pact.

Ridiculous—the day of Revelation. She'd been planning this event for years.

Beth pocketed her phone and took her coffee. Revelation would've barely been a blip on the literary radar. Now look.

There were people everywhere on the sidewalk standing or walking. On the street the snarled cars crept along. Probably not everyone was out to mourn Elizabeth Winters's death, but once a crowd gathered, others gregariously joined in.

Katie's charge of Elizabeth Winters being a publicity hound returned to him. What if she's not dead? Who was that we saw last night at the hospital? Could this all be an elaborate stunt? Might she show up at her own funeral, Huck Finn-like?

I don't know. Elaborate would hardly describe it.

A light rain began.

We'd better move along. It's likely to be a zoo getting into the Dance Center.

People on the streets were mainly somberly attired, as if deliberate mourners. Beth was a sharp contrast in her coat of winter white and light hair, a lotus blossom afloat on a murky pond. He thought of the lake scene in *Orion*, where the novelist character, Alice Rose, Elizabeth Winters's self-parody, refers to herself as Persephone, queen of the underworld. Did it imply a dark vein in the author's psyche, a tendency toward suicide? He was forever warning his students not to try too hard to connect authors' work with the authors themselves.

Nevertheless, he couldn't help himself. He began flipping

148

through a catalog of Elizabeth Winters's characters. There was the sense in "s/he" that suicide could be the fate of Toni/Tony. There is a mystery surrounding Eleanor's mother's death in "The Gold Rug," but the mother is only briefly mentioned. One of Alice Rose's grad students in *Orion* is a cutter but not suicidal per se. He could think of no one in "Pike's Peak" or "Klimt's Thread" who suggests any kind of self-harm. The protagonist of *Icarus Ascending* is stressed to the point of being frantic off and on in the book. There's Franz, the ski instructor in "Pike's Peak" who is in and out of rehab so often that the clinic director (badly) jokes they should install a revolving door just for him. Franz, however, is portrayed as more of a comic character than a tragic one.

Rain was falling harder by the time they reached the line waiting for admission to the Dance Center, still a block or so away. Beth opened her polka-dotted umbrella and they tried to take refuge beneath it, along with the bags, but it was inadequate to the task. He held his backpack out of the rain more than himself, concerned about his newly purchased book and journal.

The sidewalks and streets in the immediate vicinity were filled, in spite of the cold rain. Somberness had been replaced with an electric, near-carnival atmosphere. The death of the author had catapulted her into a celebrity status she hadn't known in life, beyond a core of devoted readers, and the increasingly weird circumstances regarding the way it happened, as they became known little by little, must have stoked the public's curiosity.

The smell of grilling sausages came to him on a gust of damp breeze. A half-block away a food truck had set up at the curb. Sausages and peppers, it seemed, and fries, espresso drinks and bottled water. They were doing a brisk business. Nearby someone was selling t-shirts beneath a temporary canvas covering. The t-shirts were either bright red with white lettering, or white with red lettering. He could make out Elizabeth Winters's name but the rest of the shirts' message was too small to read. He was sure it was unauthorized merchandising.

They progressed along the walk. Shortly they saw people standing in a half circle, intently watching some spectacle. It took a moment to process. There was a couple on the sidewalk oddly dressed for the season and the weather: he in khaki walking shorts and an Argyle sweater; she in a sky-blue pantsuit and a man's fedora, an ostrich plume protruding from its band. She was saying, . . . don't you dare use the phrase star-crossed, I swear to God—

He said, That'll be some trick, since you claim He doesn't exist, or is it postulate, *Professor*? (Professor was said sneeringly.)

Oh, are we using titles now . . . *Grad Student*?

The young man threw down the coffee cup he'd been holding. Empty. And stormed off.

The semicircular crowd and some of the Logos in line applauded appreciatively. His and Beth's hands were full. The two were actors (maybe theater majors at the university) doing a scene from *Orion*—the lovers' quarrel. The grad student came back and waved to the crowd to acknowledge their response, while his partner curtsied in her pantsuit.

Three young people dressed all in black, including berets, rushed up and handed umbrellas to the actors portraying *Dr. Sands* and *Bryan Hefferkamp*. The trio in black were The Poets of course, who function as the Fates in the novel. The First Poet, a young woman, blond ponytail, willowy, began miming climbing a ladder. She climbed in place for a full minute, always gazing upward, before The Second Poet said, You realize we're not mimes, we're poets. He was stocky, bearded, reminding him of the nurse in the ER. That's right, said The Third Poet, a woman whose reddish locks were nearly too closely cropped to see beneath her beret, our messages to the world are not so overt. They require more teasing and less certainty. Yes, like life itself, added The Second Poet. Why is that? asked The First Poet, still poised on her imaginary ladder, one black Chuck raised as if resting on a rung, hands gripping air at head level. Poets Two and Three exchanged quizzical looks, each searching for help from the other. I'm not certain, said The Second Poet scratching his beard as if absentmindedly. We must be sublime, offered The Third Poet. Must we? said The First Poet, relaxing from her pose on the ladder. Yes, said The Third. Poets must make appeal to the reader's soul more so than their mind. That's right, said The Second. We must speak in the language of the Great Mystery, the Universal Enigma. I.e., said The Third Poet, the Sublime. O.k., said The First, where was I climbing? What *specifically* was I climbing? You were climbing up, said The Second, specifically on a ladder. A ladder? That's not very specific. All right, said The Third, helping out, an extension ladder. The First shook her head in a slow emphatic no. Not even close. Well, I have to be close, said The Third. Ladders are ladders pretty much. Tell us then, please, said The Second.

Before she could reply, a voice spoke from the crowd: Jacob's Ladder. That's right, said The First Poet, vindicated. The fellow who spoke stepped forward. He was dressed as an academic, tweed coat, narrow woolen tie, but wearing a miner's helmet and carrying a pick on his padded shoulder. It was Foucault of course; this was the dream sequence from *Orion*. The poet wishes to ascend to the heavens, said Foucault (with a faltering French accent), but it is not merely for divine inspiration, to return to earth with Promethean fire. Rather, he desires to establish his dominance as the purveyor of truth and thus insinuate himself into the State apparatus, to become an instrument of control via his eloquence. Poetry as propaganda. Foucault switched on his helmet's lamp. It is a simple matter of applying the archeology, he declared, self-satisfied. Foucault balanced the miner's pick against his leg long enough to light a cigarette and inhale deeply.

Enter Baudrillard, whispered Beth. They'd been inching along in the line while watching the street performance.

Forget Foucault! railed Baudrillard from the crowd. He stepped forward, dark pants, wrinkled white dress shirt, black tie hanging stained and limp from his neck. He wore an old television, minus its insides, as a kind of helmet, his face where the screen should be, rabbit-ears as insect-like antennae, one extended farther than the other. The face inside the TV wore a thin mustache and black-rimmed glasses. Forget Foucault, he repeated (his French accent better). Old news is no news. If people no longer know the allusion it has shed its effect, like an exoskeleton to be blown away on the wind, blown to oblivion. Only the *now* matters, and it matters very little, because the *now* quickly becomes the *then* and its power is depleted to *zero*: a battery which flares once and then is immediately dead.

The residue of control remains, asserted Foucault, even if the knowledge has become obscure.

Nonsense! cried Baudrillard. I shall seduce you with the bright and beautiful moment, the sexy and sensational instant, and you shall be powerless against its empty charms. He began to loosen his tie even more and move his hips as if beginning an alluring dance. The crowd began to whistle and applaud. See? said Baudrillard from his TV helmet, an improvised line.

How dare you! seethed an indignant Foucault, tossing away his cigarette and raising the pick-ax. Baudrillard grabbed his adversary by the shoulders and they began to mock wrestle.

He and Beth moved with the line to a point where they had difficulty seeing the actors through the crowd. It was no matter. They knew how the scene ends, with a snowy-haired Derrida coming to break up the dispute. It was the critics dream sequence from *Orion*, an abridged version of it at least. In the novel the argument between Foucault and Baudrillard continues for thirty pages before erupting into a bareknuckle boxing match. It was one of the scenes in the book that made him fall in love with Elizabeth Winters. What other contemporary novelist would put such an absurd scene in their book, tailored to such a minuscule audience? A writer, it would seem, who could only achieve a wider audience postmortem—a fact which Elizabeth Winters may have understood. To what lengths would a writer go for an enthusiastic audience? Death?

Rain thrummed loudly on their shared umbrella. He imagined his purchases from Orville's were getting wet even though they were folded inside the store's plastic bag and stowed inside his backpack. It was all right. A little water damage would only add character—like a dueling scar or a trick knee from the rugby field—and prompt him to recall this moment, on the crowded sidewalk in the weather with Beth, deep within her own reverie.

He wanted to put his arm around Beth's shoulders, not as a pass or even an expression of affection, not precisely, but an attempt to stay the moment, to halt trudging time. He may have, too, had not a young woman in a yellow vest spoken to them:

You're Logos, aren't you? She may have noticed Beth's badge through her unbuttoned coat, or she knew them from the photo.

Yes, said Beth, rising from the depths of her thoughts.

Come this way. We're trying to get you all situated first.

They followed her conspicuous yellow vest out of the line, passing dozens of people who waited patiently in the rain in the hope of sitting in the back of the auditorium or at least standing.

The woman in the yellow vest led them through a door into the Dance Center's main hall. She pointed to a table. Tell them your names over there. There's a coat check down the hall. You can check your bags also. Then she went back out to collect more Logos among the mourners.

They showed their badges at the table and were given seat numbers, together this time. Then they dropped off their bags and coats, and used the bathroom. He waited in the hall for Beth. It was a familiar posture. He thought of the various places he'd stood waiting for Katie, concert halls, shopping malls, state parks, a church before a wedding ceremony (her friend's), the planetarium on their first date.

He recalled such times fondly. Certainly they were more pleasant memories than the friction over religion, and Katie's holding onto her apartment, and Elizabeth Winters's place as a writer. What did it say, that some of his best memories were waiting for her outside a bathroom?

Beth emerged, as the sound of the hand-drier spiked and faded with the closing door. She smiled, and surprised him by taking his arm. Shall we? she said.

VI

WINNOWING FAN

Young man anywhere, in whom something is welling up that makes you shiver, be grateful that no one knows you.

— Rainer Maria Rilke

Chicago 12

THEY WERE IN THE SEVENTH ROW, MORE OR LESS IN THE middle. There was a quiet energy in the auditorium. People were talking but mainly in hushed tones. It felt quite different from the shock and excitement of Revelation, only a day before. It seemed further in the past, or not real at all.

Apparently the plan was to seat the Logos in attendance first; then fill the seats and the balcony with non-Logos who'd come to pay their respects, or to indulge their curiosity.

They'd only been seated a moment when a woman of middle age, flanked by two younger women (maybe grad students at the university), walked up to the Logos section and motioned to get their attention. One grad student was holding a cardboard box. The other bore half-sheets of paper in her hand.

Thank you all for being here today, said the woman. We know many of you rearranged your travel plans to attend the memorial. We'd like to include you, Elizabeth's beloved Logos, in the program, with your help. We'll be coming around with paper and pen if you'd like to express yourself, a favorite quote or a message for Elizabeth or for Marian, whatever you like. We're also sending you a link for anyone who would prefer to share something online.

The grad students began going up and down the aisles distributing the paper to Logos with raised hands.

What the hell, said Beth signaling for a slip of paper.

He took a pen from his pocket to flag down two slips of paper, which were passed along the row, and he handed one to Beth. They were blank sheets except at the bottom Logos were encouraged to write their name and/or word.

This is a lot of pressure, he said, to be profound on the spot.

Maybe sincere is enough under the circumstances, said Beth, already concentrating.

He thought for a moment and Rilke returned to him:

You, shooting star
Who fell through my gaze, and through my body—:
Never to forget you, but endure.

He folded his slip of paper in half just as Beth was finishing too. He handed the two slips back down the row to the graduate assistant that was collecting them. He had no idea what Beth had written, but he did see that her comment was anonymous too. So even when they were posted or published somewhere, he would have no way of knowing for certain what Beth's message to Elizabeth Winters was. The mystery of Beth grew deeper every moment he spent with her: the questions and the enigmas collected together like twigs and leaves after a downpour, coming to rest at a sudden curve in the creek. In his peripheral vision Beth appeared fuzzy, out of focus, yet in many ways this was the true Beth. Looking at her straight on, seeing starkly the bend of her eyebrows, the verdure of her eyes, the slope of her nose, the line of her lips—lips he'd been thinking of kissing from almost the moment he met her—the clarity of all these features contrasted with the secret that was Beth, the unknown and unknowable Beth. It was a simple thing to paint in the missing details, using whatever hues on the palette he fancied, employing brush or blade or sponge, oil or acrylic or watercolor—creating her portrait however he saw fit, creating *her* however he

160

saw fit. Perhaps the fabricated Beth, the false Beth was the Beth he wanted, the Beth he preferred. The arcane Beth could return to Madison, to the mystery from which she'd materialized. He would keep hold of the Beth who was his rendering, his interpretation.

It was better, safer, more resilient to change: fixed in time and space.

He checked his cell to make sure it was silenced and to see the time. It was already past the start time of the memorial by a couple of minutes. He also wondered if there was a new text from Katie. There wasn't.

He recalled the summer of waiting for Katie—waiting for her to return to town to take up her teaching post in the fall. His waiting for her—not knowing if she had any feelings for him, any interest in dating him—cast those months in a kind of purity in his memory. Wanting Katie filled the void, or filled the void enough, of not being with anyone so that he could focus his thoughts and his energy. That brief time was the happiest he'd been for a long while: not just reading and writing and learning to stargaze, but being able to give those activities his full attention. Katie Sargent was a muse whose absence inspired him to enact a good version of himself, a holy version—a self something like he'd always imagined, if only vaguely.

But their relationship having become something else, he became someone else. After the initial elation, the first blush of bliss, the uncertainties began, the nagging questions about Katie and their relationship; and the creeping anxieties they provoked crept into everything: his writing, his reading, his teaching, his general sense of well-being. He would come to miss the monkish existence of the summer waiting for Katie. He missed the mere idea of Katie. The real Katie couldn't compete with her, which he knew wasn't Katie's fault. Yet her faultlessness altered nothing.

He glanced at Beth, who was looking elsewhere. Was the idea

of a life with Beth inevitably better than an actual life with Beth? Could no reality live up to the fantasy? He thought of all the failed marriages and fractured relationships—they were everywhere, in the media, in real life. Sure, there were couples who remained together, like his own parents, but were they happy? To achieve something like happiness they lived their life together practically apart, occupying their own spaces in the house, having their own interests and their own activities, even their own sets of friends.

He could think of couples who seemed truly happy together, who shared common sympathies, but they were harder to think of . . . and was the appearance of harmony just that, a façade falsifying some much different reality?

Applause interrupted his thoughts. Marian Tate had come out and gone to the podium. She was wearing a simple black dress, accented with a purple scarf. She appeared more composed, less shell-shocked than she had yesterday, understandably. Already the death of her life partner had begun to find some rational place in her psyche, some space where the knowledge of her lover's death could live without killing her. That would be the accustomed understanding. He thought of Chopin's classic "The Story of an Hour," wherein the protagonist, a woman and a wife, must hide the joy and relief she feels at finding out her husband was killed in a railroad accident. What if Elizabeth Winters had been an absolute beast to live with? What if Marian Tate's initial reaction was one of a tremendous weight being lifted?

Nothing supported that version of things . . . but how could one really know?

He glanced again at Beth, who was focused on Marian Tate, and tried to imagine a scenario in which he felt relief at the news of Beth's demise. He edited himself, removing the euphemism: news of Beth's death. It was unfathomable now—when he already felt the flowing fissures of his heart, its stability failing at the thought of his being separated from her. He could intellec-

162

tualize all he liked, and maybe ultimately it would help, but for now his heart teetered on the brink of breaking—and nothing would prevent its toppling over the edge.

. . . before we get to the memorial itself, Marian Tate was saying, I'm afraid we have a bit of business to attend to. I'm loath to begin in this mode but I'm convinced it's an important step in ensuring Elizabeth's plan, as far as we are able to know it, and so many of you beautiful Logos are gathered here—anyway, I am rambling. . . . Let me introduce Martin Townsend, Elizabeth's longtime friend and attorney. He is here in both capacities today, in many capacities.

A balding fellow in a gray suit came from the side of the stage. The suit, though expensive-looking, was a rumpled, and he appeared to be in need of a good night's sleep. It was the man from the hotel and then from the hospital.

He and Beth shared the recognition between them.

Martin Townsend stopped before the podium and spoke into the microphone. Thank you, Marian. Good afternoon, everyone. I'll try to conclude this business as quickly as possible. As Marian mentioned, I was Elizabeth's attorney and her executor, which places me in a position to try to assure her legacy. As many of you know, because you've already been approached by one entity or another, there are those who are trying to profit from Elizabeth's sudden notoriety and this morbid spike of interest in her work, and in particular this final work, *The Isolation of Conspiracy*. They are attempting to purchase the chips that Logos now bear, extract them, and work around their encryption so that as much of the novel as they can acquire will be published now—not in the next century as Elizabeth intends . . . intended. Given the unusual physicality of this book we were not able to establish its copyright. Quite honestly, Elizabeth had great faith in you, her beloved Logos, to carry out her wishes—but even the imaginative mind of Elizabeth Winters didn't foresee publishers and agents swooping in under these bizarre circumstances. I'm not sure how clearheaded Elizabeth was in her final days—

Marian Tate, who was standing off to his side, reached out and touched the attorney's shoulder: a gentle reminder to stay on track.

Yes, so . . . Martin Townsend removed a stack of paper from a shelf inside the podium. I have here a brief legal document—akin I suppose to a nondisclosure agreement—which asserts that you will abide by the author's wishes as we understand them, and not sell, gift or bequeath your portion of the manuscript, that is, your chip, prior to its planned obsolescence and retrieval. We would ask that you sign and date this single sheet of paper. We know that all Logos are not present, and we'll be seeking their agreement electronically.

Martin Townsend walked to the edge of the stage and handed stacks of the agreement to the grad student helpers. As they began distributing the paper he added, Elizabeth had tremendous faith in you, and Marian and I do too, so if you would sign and date the agreement and we'll collect them. Then the memorial, our true purpose in being here, can begin.

The assistants started handing out the forms, row by row.

This makes me uncomfortable, said Beth. I don't like signing legal documents. I don't even like clicking I Agree when downloading a new app.

I know what you mean. It somehow cheapens the project, commercializes it or something.

The assistant had counted off the number for their row, and in a moment he and Beth had their sheets in hand. The wording and its intent were as simple and as straightforward as Martin Townsend had said.

I have no intention of selling my chip, he said, so what's the harm, I suppose.

I don't either but doing something on your honor, not because of some legal agreement, makes it more meaningful. That's why there's the expression a solemn oath, not a solemn NDA.

164

He had his pen out and was poised to sign his name. Instead, on the top of the agreement he wrote Not necessary—and that was all. No signature or date.

Beth borrowed his pen and wrote the same thing on her sheet. Rebels, she said handing him back the pen.

With a cause.

They passed their unsigned forms to the Logos at the end of the row. The young man read their conspiracy and smiled at them. Then he took a moment to complete his own form.

It was going to take a few minutes for all the forms to be gathered. Meanwhile Martin Townsend stood near the podium chatting quietly with Marian Tate. They may have been discussing the impending trip to Iowa, the investigation into the crash, and the private service for Elizabeth Winters. Their long sad journey was far from complete.

What time will you need to leave to catch your train? Beth asked.

That's a good question. Normally I'd say four-thirty would be all right, but with the crazy traffic—maybe more like four. You?

I decided to stay overnight. I'd taken tomorrow off anyway. Not at the Livingstone though, someplace cheaper.

The idea of Beth staying another night in the city, without him, accelerated his sense of loss, sharpened it. He felt himself nodding, acknowledging what she'd said; he felt himself saying nothing.

Before he could not say anything further, the assistants were returning the forms to the stage. Elizabeth Winters's attorney took them, thanked everyone with a wave, then exited stage-left.

Marian Tate stood at the microphone. This weekend was intended to be one of surprises, just not the shocking ones that were in store. One of the surprises was to be for Elizabeth herself. Not many of Elizabeth's readers know that she has a sister, a twin sister in fact, an identical twin, Ellen. Elizabeth didn't think that Ellen would travel here for Revelation, didn't expect her to,

165

but she refused to miss her big sister's—Elizabeth was a minute older—her big sister's big event. Would you welcome Ellen Winters Townsend. Marian Tate stepped back and applauded warmly.

From stage-left Martin Townsend pushed a wheelchair holding Ellen Winters, his wife and Elizabeth's sister. The woman seemed very small and weak. She wore a red jacket and a tartan shawl was draped over her legs. He could see the resemblance in her face to the author but had to peer beyond the red lips and the makeup which were intended to give some appearance of life and health. Instead it seemed merely a rehearsal for the mortuary's cosmetologist. The poor woman was ill with something terrible, something crippling.

Ellen Winters Townsend raised a skeletal arm from the tartan shawl and waved to the Logos. She mouthed thank you with her thin crimson lips, smiled. Then her husband wheeled her away.

Poor woman, said Beth.

Indeed.

The mystery of the hospital visit was solved. Now the mystery shifted to how long Ellen would last before joining her sister in the hereafter.

Marian Tate continued. We know many of you, most of you have travel schedules you must adhere to—likely revised schedules so that you could attend Elizabeth's memorial tribute—so we will keep things moving along. I know Elizabeth would approve. She was not one to sit for long. Too many projects, too many ideas to sit idle. We've decided the best way to honor her—the best way to honor any writer—is with her own words.

His phone was in his shirt pocket and he kept feeling alerts vibrate against his chest—were they real or just phantoms? Figments of his heartsick imagination?

Marian Tate said, With the assistance of the university English Department, who've been wonderful by the way (I can

166

understand why Elizabeth loved her time here, loved this city), with their help three excerpts from Elizabeth's work will be read. I have no doubt they will be familiar to Logos. Now they will take on special meaning given the place and time and each reader's unique interpretation. As you know, Elizabeth had a particular interest in the life of text once it began to interact with readers. Marian Tate laughed self-consciously. This is an audience, of course, which understands that better than anyone about Elizabeth.

She shuffled some pages on the podium. Please welcome first of all Doctor Cynthia Hobson, English professor emerita, who was Elizabeth's senior thesis adviser. As you probably know, Elizabeth's senior thesis eventually evolved into the prose poetry collection *The Gadgets of God*, published by Shimmering Shadows Press as the winner of the Teasdale Prize. It so happens that Cynthia still has in her possession the thesis draft of "Winnowing Fan," the collection's introductory piece. Hoarders of the world unite! As you will hear, it is the same but yet subtly different in important ways from the published version.

Cynthia Hobson came to the podium as the Logos applauded politely. She was silver-haired and wiry and walked as loosely and as lightly as any of the young grad students who milled around the Dance Center like worker ants. She wore a long floral scarf over a gray sheath dress. The scarf, principally orange and yellow, was looped over one shoulder like a cape that had become eschew in a scuffle. She held a leather-clad e-reader. When she arrived at the podium, she angled the microphone downward and peered over the top of her owlish, purple-framed glasses:

Good afternoon, Logos. I am so grateful to be asked here to honor Lizzie. Thirty-some years later I recall so warmly and so vividly our tête-à-têtes over coffee discussing her thesis. No offense to my other students—I love you all—but these meetings with Lizzie are among my happiest teaching memories. She was so filled with energy and wit and charm, just being around her

167

was intoxicating, invigorating. Without further delay, an excerpt from the thesis draft of "Winnowing Fan."

Cynthia Hobson adjusted her large glasses and began reading. Her pacing was slow, her voice subtly dramatic. It'd been a long while since he'd read the piece. He recalled that the title was an allusion to Homer's *Odyssey*, having to do with Odysseus' already leaving home again shortly after his epic homecoming. Elizabeth Winters's piece had nothing to do with Homer's poem directly. It was about the inevitability of change, the inevitability of a person being true to their nature no matter how badly they may wish to behave like someone else, to be someone else.

Cynthia Hobson read a sentence which resonated with him in particular:

Your beloved had been razed and raised to the hollowest and most hallowed holds in your heart through a mere trick of perspective. Now you must decide how to see.

As he thought about Elizabeth Winters's words, felt them again rush through his psyche like a moonlit wave, he believed he sensed the impossible vibration of an alert against his chest. At the same moment he felt Beth's hand clasp his. Their fingers interlocked like designed pieces. Neither looked at the other, as if the handholding were an accident, or as if it were as natural as the ebbing and flowing of tides.

The phantom impulses continued to pound against his chest, against his heart. Could he have left notifications on? And Katie was desperately trying to reach him?

With his free hand he removed his phone from his shirt pocket, under the projected pretense of checking the time. There were alerts but only one message: his train was running on time—the train that would speed him away from Beth was, of course, a model of efficiency and punctuality. He felt the Fates conspiring against him, like carefully synchronized thieves plotting a coldhearted theft.

Cynthia Hobson concluded her reading, and the next speaker was introduced: Anton Bree, who was known internationally for their advocacy of transgender rights and was a celebrity in the city, according to Marian Tate's introduction. He thought perhaps he'd heard of Anton Bree, who didn't know Elizabeth Winters personally but had been inspired by "s/he" as a teen growing up on the South Side. Please welcome them, said Marian Tate.

Anton Bree stepped from the curtain. They were heavyset and dressed all in black, black well-tailored suit, black shirt, highly polished black leather shoes. No tie. Anton Bree held rolled pages like a scroll. They shunned the microphone and stepped to the edge of the stage. They began reciting a passage from "s/he" from memory. Anton Bree slapped the scroll against the palm of their hand in time to the beat of Elizabeth Winters's prose:

The girlboy walked until overtaken by exhaustion and finding a park lay in a space where greengrass was trampled by day by picnickers and children at play. By dogs domesticated and animals of the field.

Anton Bree's voice was sonorous and hypnotic and took full advantage of the auditorium's perfect acoustics. They continued reciting the scene in which the protagonist lies awake in the park in utter darkness save for the stars glittering in the moonless sky. The description of the night sounds mixed with recollections of the protagonist's past was considered by some to be Elizabeth Winters's most lyrical prose. Predawn birdsong seems to signal a coming resolve to embrace Tony's/Toni's true nature, neither male nor female, gay or straight—but human. Anton Bree concluded,

Humanity alternately soft and alternately spiked, sometimes gay and sometimes straight, bearer of a kindness veined with cruelty—offered a cheek to kiss in greeting, in welcome, and in good-bye, a cool cheek whose capacity to receive warmth remained to be seen. But Toni would see . . . gray dawn began to gift color to the new day.

Anton Bree's scroll quietly beat their palm on the stroke of day. The Logos applauded wildly as Anton Bree exited the stage.

Powerful, said Beth, squeezing his hand a degree tighter.

He smiled to her in agreement and returned her added pressure. Yet it was as if their clasped hands were beings unto themselves, somehow separated from him and Beth—and he couldn't read them, couldn't decode what they meant. The hands were like extraterrestrial creatures who may have been engaged in some kind of courtship or an embrace that was prelude to sparring or something so alien there was hardly its equivalent in the human catalog. Only an awkward approximation.

Marian Tate was at the podium again,

. . . may be familiar to you. I've been requested to simply introduce them as The Poets.

No one came from either side of the stage. Enough time elapsed that it seemed perhaps something was wrong. Then there was a stir among the Logos. He and Beth turned—to do so they had to release their hands—and The Poets, all in black including their black berets, were approaching the stage via the aisles. They were the same young people who'd performed on the sidewalk. The First Poet, the willowy blonde with the ponytail, was to his and Beth's left. The Second Poet, the dark-bearded young man, was to their right. The Third Poet, with the short-shorn red curls, was not in view.

First Poet: Is the past prologue? And therefore the future, what? Epilogue? And the now?

Second Poet: Logos. The present is constructed of Logos. Ev-

170

ery moment is made of language, wired together with words.

First Poet: Which came first? The chicken or the word chicken?

Second Poet: Clearly the word chicken preceded chicken as concept. One couldn't speak of chicken, conceive of chicken, before language created it . . . from thin air. Chicken, pollo, poulette, Hänchen, sicín, frango.

First Poet: But could one roast the concept? Combine the concept with dumplings? Pair it with a nicely chilled Chablis? Could one collect the concept's eggs and scramble them into a rosemary and thyme omelet? Were not cavepeople picking chicken from between their crooked teeth before they could wax eloquent on the culinary pros and cons? Chicken, say, versus quail?

The Poets now stood before the stage, facing the audience. He thought of holding Beth's hand again but her hands were folded in her lap. He hadn't felt this awkward, this foolish since high school. He knew it appeared rude but he took out his phone to check the time: 4:07 . . . and he had a text. Maybe his train was delayed. This time, Katie: Let's talk when you get back. He glanced at Beth. She seemed captivated by the performance, not a care in the world.

He had missed a line or two. Everyone's laughing retrieved his attention. The Third Poet had finally appeared, on stage, slowly strutting about like a chicken, arms bent into wings, head bobbing, black ballet-slippered toes scratching at the stage floor. Clucking. Still strutting, she said:

What am I?

Neither Poet wanted to answer; it was a trap. Finally,

Second Poet: A chicken.

Third Poet: I bet I'll be tasty with some dumplings. (She shook her hind feathers.)

First Poet: I think the Logos machine may be broken. Instead of making a chicken, the word chicken made a clown.

Second Poet: (grumbling) More accurately a fool.

Logos broke into laughter again, which he used as cover. He stood and began moving toward the aisle, pardoning himself person by person. He glanced toward Beth, who was watching his departure. He mouthed the word sorry. Her expression was inscrutable.

Once free of the row, he hurried out of the auditorium. The sound of The Poets, the Fates, receded; the laughter they evoked faded.

He retrieved his coat and backpack from the coatroom. He thought Beth might pursue him, to say good-bye properly at least. She had not. Possibly she was as confused and as shaken as he was. Possibly more so. After all, she was the one who had taken his hand. Hadn't she? It had only happened minutes ago, and yet he couldn't say exactly what took place. He was definitely the one who fled from the auditorium without so much as a word to her, a spoken word anyway.

On the street the rain was falling harder, which had helped to disperse the carnivalesque crowd of mourners, or at least the morbidly curious. Journalists were still on the sidewalk outside the Dance Center, laying wait here and there. His leaving the building caught them by surprise. One or two made an effort to speak with him but he rushed past, and his manner preempted any others from bothering. Had he stopped, he wouldn't have known what to say.

A block away an impromptu cabstand had formed. He half jogged in the cold rain to secure a taxi. He slid into the back of a red and white cab. Train station. And the cabby pulled away from the curb. He looked back for a moment to see if Beth was hurrying after him. The rain was hastening night in the city, and in the gray light he saw only the steadfast journalists, their microphones and cameras sheathed in plastic, and a few curious stragglers, who may have been just ordinary pedestrians out on a miserable evening.

He tried to make small talk with the cab driver but she was focused on speeding and running red lights, which she treated like inconveniently placed yield signs. Her goal was to drop him at the station as quickly as possible so that she could return to the Dance Center for more fares.

He set back and tried to be entertained by the spectacle of her outrageous driving, zooming around cars that had the right-of-way and honking at pedestrians to stay put if they valued their lives. They all did, and he was at the station in no time, a full twenty-five minutes before his train was to depart. He fumbled a bit with the taxi's card-reader, much to the impatient cabby's dismay. Then he was in the rain again, on the sidewalk, getting his bearings. He entered the labyrinthine station and looked for the signs to the correct gates. He was watchful, in fact, for any signs.

He had to go down a level. His backpack was noticeably heavier with the new purchases. He thought of the journal and its blank pages, and of filling them with words—and not just any words, but the right words, the ones he was meant to write. Everything, everyone had led him to this moment: Elizabeth Winters, Katie Sargent, Beth Winterberry, Frannie Franks . . . the homicidal taxi driver, even the woman on the public-address system whose voice was instructing him that his train was beginning to board.

Ahead, he saw the line forming at the designated gate. The passengers were weary, and they wore their impatience like a suit of heavy-plate armor.

The first words he would write came to him, but they were not for his journal, not yet at least. He took out his phone. He had no signal in the catacomb-like structure of the station. He watched the ragtag line of passengers inching along, directed to the correct platform for boarding his train.

He turned away from the gate and began thumb-typing a message. Rushing travelers had to beware of him. He barely reg-

173

istered their annoyed looks.

He came to the station's escalator and let it carry him upward, a kind of mechanical apotheosis. He passed a group going down he recognized from the previous day: the medievalists, now with broken lances and battered shields. One lady wore a conical hat that was crushed crooked and trailing a torn veil. It must have been a brutal fair. By the time he reached the upper level, a wave-borne signal found his phone. He launched his message into the ether, where it would be bounced to another phone, let loose from the heavens as if a fated prophecy.

It was a simple request—

Could you take my class tomorrow. 11. Topic, the audience is always unknowable. Thanx iou

There was a Twitter alert: @E_Winterberry was now following him.

He went to a coffee place in the station. It was mostly empty. He bought a cup of their darkest roast and sat at a small table. He unpacked his new journal and pen. The cover of the journal was slightly damp. He opened to the first page, which was as blankly white as the city had been, and he began to write.

174

About the Author

Ted Morrissey's novels include *Mrs Saville* (Manhattan Book Award) and *Crowsong for the Stricken* (International Book Award and American Fiction Award). His stories, novel excerpts, poems, essays and reviews have appeared in approximately eighty publications. A lecturer in Lindenwood University's MFA in Writing program, he and his wife Melissa, also an author and educator, live near Springfield, Illinois. In 2012, he founded Twelve Winter Press, modeling it after Leonard and Virginia Woolf's Hogarth Press.

tedmorrissey.com – @t_morrissey – *FB* jtedmorrissey

www.ingramcontent.com/pod-product-compliance
Lightning Source LLC
Chambersburg PA
CBHW032008170626
46807CB00006B/2701

9781733194938